Ryan had to resist putting his arms around her.

He settled for lightly tipping his chin up so he could look straight into those soft brown eyes. "It's going to be all right."

She nodded, but her eyes betrayed her fright. He was startled by a suddenly overwhelming need to protect her at all costs. More than that, he realized he wanted to draw her close and kiss those trembling lips. His gaze must have dropped to her lips, but instead of pulling away from his touch, her mouth seemed to part slightly with anticipation.

Then she suddenly did pull back as they heard a noise in the hall. And without much more warning than that, they were back to business.

Before turning away, she hesitated as if she wanted to say something more. Then she headed for the door.

"Good night, then," he said, but all she gave him in return was a quick nod. And then she was gone.

The moment was over.

LEONA KARR

SILENT WITNESS

HARLEQUIN®

TORONTO • NEW YORK • LONDON
AMSTERDAM • PARIS • SYDNEY • HAMBURG
STOCKHOLM • ATHENS • TOKYO • MILAN • MADRID
PRAGUE • WARSAW • BUDAPEST • AUCKLAND

To Leslie Pitz and Angela Hart, with thanks for their help,
encouragement and love.

ISBN-13: 978-0-373-88830-6
ISBN-10:   0-373-88830-9

SILENT WITNESS

www.eHarlequin.com

Printed in U.S.A.

ABOUT THE AUTHOR

A native of Colorado, Leona Karr lives near the front range of the Rocky Mountains. She delights in being close to craggy cliffs, dramatic peaks and hidden valleys. It is no surprise, then, that she chooses this setting for many of her books. She has been on the Waldenbooks bestseller list and received many awards as a multipublished author of novels of romantic suspense, gothic, historical romance, time travel and mystery.

Books by Leona Karr

HARLEQUIN INTRIGUE
574—INNOCENT WITNESS
623—THE MYSTERIOUS TWIN
672—LOST IDENTITY
724—SEMIAUTOMATIC MARRIAGE
792—A DANGEROUS INHERITANCE
840—SHADOWS ON THE LAKE
900—STONEVIEW ESTATE
949—CHARMED
973—SHADOW MOUNTAIN
1056—SILENT WITNESS

CAST OF CHARACTERS

Marian Richards—Director of the summer program for deaf children.

Ryan Darnell—Detective at Rock Creek Police Department.

Scotty Tanner—The eleven-year-old rebellious boy attending the summer program who may have witnessed a murder.

Alva Wentworth—Wealthy elderly owner of Wentworth mansion and estate.

Ruth Tilman—Officious personal secretary to Alva Wentworth.

Henry Ziller—Cantankerous caretaker of Wentworth estate.

Victor Blaise—Henry's nephew is both transient and dangerous.

Toby Bower—Forensic detective at Rock Creek Crime Laboratory.

Arthur Kennedy—The Denver lawyer hired to oversee the summer program may have come with his own agenda.

Nancy Collins and Ron Harman—Teachers involved with the summer program.

Bertha Higgins—Motherly nurse who helps children in the summer program.

Elsie Mullens—Wentworth estate cook, who is both outgoing and friendly.

Joyce Phillips—Is Ryan's attractive ex trying to stir up trouble?

Prologue

Hidden in a thick drift of pine and cedar trees, Scotty Tanner didn't hear the shot inside the mountain cabin even though a sharp gunfire report echoed loudly from the house. A chatter of blue jays in a nearby ponderosa pine went unheard as he waited and watched. Nothing but stillness dominated the deaf eleven-year-old boy's world.

Scotty was spending the summer with a dozen other hearing-impaired children in a privately sponsored rehabilitation program held on a large mountain estate near Rock Creek, Colorado. He'd only been there for a week and had managed to duck out of most of the scheduled activities. He was patting himself on the back for slipping away right after lunch to investigate the mountain surroundings on his own.

About a half mile downstream from the

large main house and outbuildings, he'd discovered a small cabin built near a swift-flowing mountain stream.

As he slowly moved out of the trees, his eyes darted in every direction.

No sign of anyone living in the place. No telling what kind of loot was waiting inside.

His heart jumped a beat as he boldly walked up the front steps. Shuffling nervously, he knocked on the door. He was glad he was good at reading lips and was ready with a lie about needing a drink of water if anyone opened it.

He'd lost his hearing a couple of years ago when he was running with a gang of older guys and had been experimenting with homemade bombs. One of them had gone off prematurely, injuring both his ears. Things had gone from bad to worse after that. He'd been made a ward of the court and the authorities took him away from his drug-addicted mother. Hating the close supervision and boring daily routines of foster care, he intended to make the most of this summer program for disadvantaged hearing-impaired kids. He'd go his own way and get some kicks this summer any way he could.

When no one responded to his knock,

Scotty tried the door. Locked. Maybe he'd have more luck with a back door. A narrow deck circled the cabin and he quickly made his way around to a rear door flanked by two windows.

It was locked. Now what? What about a window? Both of them were locked, too, but he was able to remove one of the screens.

He hurriedly found a rock big enough to use as a sledge and used it to shatter the window glass. Carefully and swiftly, he removed the jagged shards and then hoisted himself through the opening into a small kitchen.

Inside, he hunched down in a waiting position, motionless and animal alert for any sign of danger. In the enveloping silence, he knew he had to depend entirely on sight to alert him. There would be no sounds to tell him what lay ahead, behind or beyond his peripheral vision.

Scotty could feel the skin on his neck prickling. He was alone in his silent world—*or was he? Was some second sense warning him?* As he fought the temptation to turn and bolt out the window, an inner voice mocked him. *You turning into some yellow-bellied coward?*

Straightening up and clenching his fists, he walked into the center of the kitchen and looked around. He opened some of the cupboards but didn't see anything of interest. He couldn't believe his luck when he spied an ashtray on the table with three long cigarette butts. He'd been dying for a smoke. He carefully put the butts in the pocket of his shirt and looked around for some matches but didn't see any.

Then a portable radio sitting on the counter caught his attention. For a moment he forgot his deafness and reached for it. Then the truth stabbed him! Never again would he hear rap music blaring out of a radio station.

With childish fury and frustration, he lifted the radio over his head and threw it on the floor. Then, with a vicious kick he sent it sailing across the room.

It wasn't fair. It wasn't fair!

He knocked over two chairs, swept the counters clean, spilling objects all over the floor. Then stepping over the shattered and broken clutter, he left the kitchen through a doorway that opened into a front living room. Pressing up against one wall, he waited until he was satisfied that it was as empty as the kitchen.

Boldly he moved forward to see what he might find that was worth lifting. If he was lucky, he might even find a full pack of cigarettes and a lighter.

He had just taken a few steps into the room and was looking around, when he froze with sudden terror. Lying on the floor in front of the fireplace was the crumpled body of a man. His chest was bloody and his dead eyes stared straight at Scotty.

In that paralyzing moment, a shadow flickered across the front window, warning Scotty that someone was outside near the front door.

Frantically, he bolted back to the kitchen and pushed himself out the broken window. As he scrambled to his feet, he felt vibrations on the deck boards, warning him that someone was coming around the house.

He ran as fast as he could for the nearby cover of trees, not knowing if someone right behind him might be yelling, "Stop or I'll shoot!"

Chapter One

As Marian Richards entered a large reception room in the Wentworth mansion, a hum of childish voices greeted her. The spacious, high-ceilinged room had been turned into an activity center, and as director of a summer program for disadvantaged hearing-impaired children, Marian was learning the hard way that the mountain estate with its imposing three-storied mansion had never been meant for a dozen eight- to twelve-year-old youngsters.

The property belonged to Alva Wentworth, a widow in her late seventies who was in a local nursing home. Located near one of the state's popular tourist areas in southern Colorado the estate was worth a fortune and ripe for development. Countless investors had tried to persuade the wealthy widow to sell the estate but she had stubbornly held on to it. Her only heir had been a grandson,

Stanley, whom she'd disinherited when she'd discovered a series of illegal maneuvers of his to get his hands on her money before she died. Everyone was amazed when she agreed to let the Colorado Foundation for Disadvantaged Children use the mansion and grounds for a children's summer program.

Marian was determined that everything would go smoothly under her leadership. She'd been assistant director at a private school for the hearing impaired when she heard about the summer program and quickly applied for the position. She was delighted and slightly surprised when she was offered the job even though she was the youngest applicant, only thirty years old and still working on a doctorate in social services. She was determined that all would go smoothly, because this experience would be a professional stepping stone to the position of director at one of Colorado's larger institutions.

Her first challenge had been to evaluate recommended children for the program. After considerable debate with teachers and social workers, she had chosen six boys and six girls of various ages and problems. She'd met with some negative reaction when she'd chosen Scotty Tanner, an eleven-year-old who had both hearing and emotional problems. Even his foster parents had warned her that the boy didn't do well in groups.

As Marian entered the activity room, she looked around for Scotty but didn't see the slender boy with unruly blond hair and snapping blue eyes. He usually dominated the Ping-Pong table, furiously venting his anger upon the small ball. Already Marian had learned that Scotty was constantly warring against the acceptance of his deafness and striking out at anything and everybody. He seemed intent upon isolating himself beyond what a hearing loss would create.

Uneasiness began to stir as she walked over to Rob Harman, a middle-aged physical-education teacher who had raised a deaf son and spent his summers working with the handicapped. He was easygoing and patient but at the same time firm enough to maintain control.

Marian had a staff of five people, counting herself, and was pleased they'd developed a summer curriculum that was both instructive and recreational.

"I don't see Scotty in the room, Rob. Do you know where he is?"

"He was here right after lunch but complained his stomach hurt. He asked to go back upstairs to his bunk but I sent him to the nurse. I decided Bertha could tell whether he was goldbricking or not." Rob sighed. "He's not the most sociable kid on the block."

Marian nodded in agreement. "A real loner, for sure."

The only time the boy seemed visible was when there was trouble of some kind, but she was willing to give Scotty some leeway. He'd been running the streets most of his life. No father in the picture and a mother strung out on drugs most of the time. Scotty might have ended up serving time in a juvenile facility if a homemade bomb hadn't plunged him into deafness and made him a ward of the court.

"Maybe after a few weeks in the program we'll see a change for the better," Marian told Rob. She was encouraged because she'd seen one good sign already in his behavior. For some inexplicable reason, the tough, streetwise Scotty had appointed himself protector of Mindy Simpson, a small, shy eight-year-old girl who had been deaf since birth.

Scotty had met her in class for the hearing impaired which he'd been required to attend when he was turned over to the court. It was because of the dark-haired, curly-headed Mindy that Scotty had mastered any sign language at all. Unfortunately, he seemed only willing to try signing in order to communicate with the shy little girl. Most of the time he got along as best he could with lip-reading, defying all orders to practice communicating with any of the other students.

"I'll check with the nurse," Marian told Rob and then walked across the room to a table where several girls were involved in an activity of following directions. They were making Indian god's eyes out of yarn and sticks. Because a field trip was planned to the nearby Mesa Verde Indian ruins, the teachers had decided to incorporate some of the activities, stories and art around an Indian theme.

Nancy Collins, a chubby, round-faced teacher in her early forties, was busily moving around the table, smiling, nodding and signing her approval. Marian had worked with Nancy before and was delighted when the outgoing, good-natured teacher had applied for the summer program. Together they had developed a program of activities to help hearing-impaired children develop language, speech and listening skills.

Marian stopped at Mindy's chair and

lightly touched the little girl on the shoulder to get her attention. As she looked up, her smiling eyes were a sparkling blue and full of life.

"I'm looking for Scotty," Marian signed. "Do you know where he is?"

She shook her head and her fingers flitted like butterflies as she responded, "I haven't seen him since lunch. Is he in trouble again?"

I hope not. Marian sighed silently as she nodded approval of the rather lopsided god's eye that Mindy held up for her approval.

Even though a building uneasiness urged Marian to find Scotty as soon as possible, she took time to look at all the girls' handiwork. Marian knew these children wanted so much to connect with other people that sometimes they were like puppies willing to do anything for a pat on the head.

"We're going to make one to hang in your office," Nancy told her with a grin. "It'll keep all the problems away from your door."

"What a lovely idea. The sooner the better."

"What's happening?"

"I feel as if I'm holding on to a dozen horses going in all directions," Marian admitted. "New-job jitters, I guess."

"Relax, everything's under control," Nancy assured her with her usual optimistic grin.

Marian gave her a grateful smile as she left the room and headed down the hall to a small sitting room that had been changed into a nursing station and dispensary.

Bertha Higgins was a large, motherly-looking woman in her fifties who was not only a registered nurse but also a certified teacher, trained in speech, auditory development, sign language and lip-reading. Marian had hired her because she was qualified to take turns relieving Nancy and Rob with the students so the two teachers might have some free time. When Bertha wasn't tending to medical needs or handling a class, she took it upon herself to instruct individual students about specific health habits they were ignoring.

Marian knew Bertha had playfully threatened to wash Scotty's ears and neck for him. Much to everyone's surprise the boy had given her a big grin as if he wasn't used to anyone paying that much attention to him.

Maybe he was just faking the stomachache so he could get Bertha's attention again, Marian thought as she politely knocked on the door.

"Come in."

The nurse had her back to the door, putting some medical supplies in a cabinet. When she turned around, she gave Marian a cheery smile as she said, "What can I do you for?"

"I'm looking for Scotty."

"I haven't seen him. Was he supposed to check in with me?"

"Well, Rob excused him and told him to see you because Scotty said he had a stomachache."

Bertha chuckled. "The oldest ploy in the world. Better than a headache. I bet he knows every trick in the book, that one. He's probably stretched out on his bunk waiting for dinnertime. I bet the kid's been starved a lot of his life. He'll put on a pound or two while he's here."

"Well, if he's hiding out, I just might find a job or two that will help his appetite." As she turned to leave, she said, "If he shows up, hold on to him."

"Will do."

Heading down the hall, Marian intended to go up to the second floor where the boys had assigned beds, but another youngster, Peter, came bounding down the center staircase just as she reached it.

Putting out her hand, she stopped him.

Knowing the ten-year-old was a good lip-reader, she looked straight at him and carefully mouthed her words, slowly and evenly. "Peter, did you see Scotty upstairs?"

He shook his head. "Nobody up there. I went to get this," he told her in a flat but understandable tone as he held out a small electronic game. "You want to play?"

"Not now, Peter. Maybe later," she answered.

He nodded to show he understood and then bounded down the hall toward the activity room.

Marian decided to check the kitchen, since Scotty had already been caught stealing food between meals. The cook, Elsie Mullens, had threatened him with a week's dish-washing detail if he did it again and Marian had approved the promised punishment.

She liked the hefty, gray-haired cook who had been hired to prepare the meals. Once, Marian had heard Elsie on the phone arguing with a Denver dietician about the menus they had sent her to prepare. Elsie had spent most of her life cooking for ranchers and was used to preparing meals for hardworking men with healthy appetites and not finicky youngsters.

"Yeah, he was here," Elsie replied when

Marian asked her if she'd seen Scotty. "Hanging around, he was, waiting for me to turn my back. He's got sticky fingers, that one. Lordy, he's snitched more than one pastry right out from under my nose." As she talked she vigorously patted flour on a bread board and wheeled a rolling pin over fresh dough. "I shooed him out of here fast like."

"Do you know where he went?"

Elsie shrugged her solid shoulders. "He left by the back door."

Marian mentally groaned. She knew it wasn't Elsie's duty to supervise the kids, but she wished the cook had stopped him. It wasn't an easy job to supervise all the activities inside the house. One kid like Scotty could create a crisis in spite of their best efforts. Making certain none of the children wandered off was a number-one priority. She'd have to talk to Rob about not letting any of the children run around unsupervised, even for a few minutes.

"If the kid shows up again, I'll sit him down till you come after him," Elsie promised as if she'd read Marian's mind.

"Yes, please do." Marian thanked her and left quickly by the back door.

As she stood on the top step of the wide

back porch and surveyed the surrounding foothills carpeted with thick drifts of ever-green trees, her chest tightened. She'd had enough experience in her hiking club to know how treacherous climbing slopes like those could be. A small city boy scrambling up the side of the rock-strewn slopes could easily lose his footing. Steep cliffs fell away to a swift-flowing mountain stream border-ing one edge of the property, and in her mind's eye, Marian unwittingly pictured Scotty tumbling into the current. He'd be swept downstream and—

Stop it!

Taking a deep breath, she stilled her rising apprehension and vivid imagination.

I can handle this!

She'd been telling herself that every time a crisis arose that demanded her attention and decision. The heavy responsibility of being in charge had come home to her the minute the busload of children had unloaded at the front door. Her intense week of preparation at the house to get ready seemed inadequate for the instant demands put upon her with their arrival.

Almost immediately, a myriad of unex-pected problems challenged her on every level, none of which resembled those she'd experienced in her former administrative position at the day school. Scotty Tanner was one of those challenges. It was imperative that she get the belligerent boy under control without delay.

She left the porch and quickly made a circle walking around the stone mansion. No sign of him standing on the flagstone terrace nor on the wide-veranda front porch.

A large garage stood at the end of the driveway. She peeked in and saw a couple of cars and one pickup truck. Some old bicycles and garden equipment were stored there. No sign of Scotty.

Maybe the caretaker, Henry Ziller, had seen the boy snooping around. The older, rugged, sharp-tongued man lived in the apartment above the garage and it was clear he was less than pleased about having a dozen kids running all over the place.

She knew Henry had been with the Wentworth family since his youth and was very possessive about the property. Already there had been problems about letting the children play in certain places on the grounds and he'd raised a fuss about having any play equipment scattered about.

She quickly climbed the outside stairs to the small apartment and knocked on the door.

No response. A knot in her chest began to tighten. What now? There were a hundred places in the mansion alone where a small boy could hide and enjoy the uproar of people looking for him. She wanted to do her best to make sure Scotty wasn't somewhere on the grounds or in the mansion before she organized an official search party. The uproar that would cause was something she couldn't even bear to think about.

The only places left to look on the immediate property were a small barn and stable built a short distance from the back of the house and almost hidden by stands of cedar and pine trees. She knew horses had not been stabled there for several years but maybe Scotty was scouting these empty buildings like a hopeful pack rat.

As she headed across a green meadow in the direction of the buildings, she brushed back a strand of reddish-blond hair and shaded her eyes from the bright sunlight. At first she thought her eyes were betraying her when she glimpsed a shadowy movement in the trees. She stopped and shaded her eyes with her hands. A moment later, she glimpsed a small figure running into the stable.

Scotty! Thank heavens!

Was he trying to hide from her? At the moment, she didn't know what kind of discipline was appropriate, but she was determined to make sure this kind of thing didn't happen again. Even as she cautioned herself not to lose her temper, she knew she was way too uptight for any game of hide-and-seek.

The stable door was ajar and as she stepped inside, the interior was dark and smelly. Shadowy horse stalls stretched the length of the building on both sides. As she stood there searching for any flicker of movement, a hushed, dusty silence greeted her.

She knew calling out Scotty's name was a wasted effort. If the deaf boy wasn't looking in her direction, he wouldn't even know she was there. Once more, if he was deliberately hiding from her, he wouldn't give himself away. The open stable door and small windows at both ends of the stable were the only source of a feeble light.

As she walked past the stalls, she could see inside each one because the half doors were hanging open.

All the stalls were empty.

She saw a door ajar on one side of the stable that looked as if it might open into a tack room. Maybe that's where Scotty was hiding. She pushed the door fully open and stepped inside.

A high narrow window gave shadowy light to the small room and she could see bridles and harnesses hanging from ceiling hooks. Saddles of various kinds were mounted on wooden racks and a long table was loaded with ropes, saddle blankets and various tool kits. It was obvious to Marian from the stacks of boxes and clutter that the room was being used for storage now that there were no horses stabled there.

As she looked around, her gaze settled on some feed sacks piled in one corner. At first she thought her eyes were playing tricks on her when they registered the slight movement as a small head ducked down behind one of the sacks.

Scotty! Instant relief sped through her. She'd found him! Everything was under control. She'd lay down firm rules and consequences and keep a tighter rein on him. Since she'd gone out on a limb to include Scotty in the program, no one needed to know about this little escapade.

When she pulled away one of the sacks, she exposed his cowering body and was stunned by the look of terror that flashed in his eyes. She realized the boy was trembling with fright. Her anger quickly dissipated.

"It's all right, Scotty," she mouthed as she bent close enough for him to read her lips. "Nothing bad is going to happen."

He shook his head in denial. His eyes were wide and filled with fear.

"I'm not going to punish you." She guessed that he was probably expecting the kind of discipline heaped on him by an abusive father and drug-addicted mother. No wonder his first reaction was to hide from any authority figure. "We'll talk. Now let's go back to the house."

"No."

He drew back and she wasn't prepared for this kind of rebellion. "What do you mean, no? You'll do as I say."

His fearful eyes darted to the door of the tack room. "Have to hide."

Hide? What was he talking about? He'd been hiding from her and she'd found him.

"Why do you have to hide, Scotty?" She mouthed the question with deliberate slowness.

"They might find me!"

As she searched his fearful expression, she realized he hadn't been hiding from her. Maybe he hadn't even seen her coming toward the stable. "Who might find you, Scotty?"

"The one who did it." He grabbed her hand and held on to it as if some unseen hands were trying to pull him away from her.

As the terrified eleven-year-old boy clung to her, she knew with sickening certainty he wasn't making something up. No child could pretend the kind of fear she saw in his eyes.

"The one who did what, Scotty?"

He swallowed hard. "Killed the man."

"What man, Scotty? Tell me where you were."

"The small house…by the creek," he mumbled.

She knew there was a log cabin on the estate about a mile downstream. A kind of guesthouse. As far as she knew, the place wasn't being used this summer.

"You were inside the little house?"

"But I didn't take nothing," he said with a rush.

"Tell me exactly what you did do, Scotty. Everything."

He kept his hand in hers as he told her about breaking a window, trashing the kitchen and going to hunt for some loot in the rest of the house.

"Then I saw the dead man and ran." He fixed terrified eyes on her face. "I ran before they caught me."

"Who, Scotty? Who was there?"

He shook his head.

"Are you sure there was someone?"

He raised tear-filled eyes to hers. "I felt them coming around the house. The boards moved. We have to hide."

"No, Scotty," she said with a sickening plunge of her stomach. "We have to call the police."

Chapter Two

The Rock Creek Police Department was a stone building just off Main Street. Detective Ryan Darnell was sitting at a scarred desk in his small office when the switchboard relayed a call to him. At first, Ryan didn't understand exactly what kind of crime the woman was reporting.

"My name is Marian Richards. I'm the director of an outreach program for hearing-impaired children. We are in residence at the Wentworth estate for the summer. I have a situation here that I need you to look into as soon as possible."

"Yes, ma'am," he replied. He had heard something about old lady Wentworth letting some nonprofit foundation use the property. Apparently she'd hired a female executive to run it. Ryan pictured the caller as a middle-aged, uptight spinster used to ordering people around.

"What kind of situation would that be?" he asked, leaning back in his chair. He wasn't about to drive five miles up a canyon road because some authoritative director didn't want to take care of some piddling matter.

"I think there may have been a crime committed on the property."

"You don't know for sure?" Ryan's tone was slightly mocking.

"No, I don't. That's why I'm calling you," she replied impatiently. "I need someone to investigate."

"What kind of crime are we talking about?"

"I'm not sure…maybe murder."

Ryan's chair came forward with a thump. "Murder!"

AS RYAN DROVE to the Wentworth estate up the mountain road winding through Prospect Canyon, he had the feeling he was wasting his time. The three-story stone mansion and extensive property had been vacant for over a year and he was curious who had persuaded Alva Wentworth, a wealthy widow, to let a charitable foundation use it for the summer. He'd heard that a Denver lawyer, Arthur

Kennedy, who was overseeing the project, had been paying regular visits to Alva in a Rock Creek nursing home. Apparently there weren't any legal problems turning the estate into a retreat for children with hearing problems, but Ryan was willing to bet the isolated rugged property would create plenty of headaches for those in charge of the program. He just hoped this wouldn't include a series of SOS calls to the Rock Creek Police Department.

A simple sign, Private Property, identified a fork in the road and Ryan took the one that wound through thick stands of ponderosa pine and aspens. In about a quarter of a mile, an open gate to the estate came into view.

Even though Ryan had been there on some occasions during his growing-up years in Rock Creek, he still found the stone mansion set against the backdrop of rising mountain slopes very impressive.

As he drove the police car to the front entrance, he saw a woman and a scowling boy sitting on the steps. Obviously waiting for him, they stood up as he got out of the police car.

Ryan's mental picture of Marian Richards underwent an immediate revision. She was young and pretty enough to attract his attention under any circumstances. Reddish-blond hair fell softly around her face and a soft green summer dress revealed a feminine figure that could have graced any fashion magazine.

"Thank you for coming, Detective," she said as she walked down the front steps to meet him. "I'm Marian Richards."

Something in the way her glance swept over him gave the impression that she was expecting someone older and wearing a uniform instead of casual brown slacks and a summer knit pullover open at the neck. He only wore a jacket when it was necessary to hide a shoulder holster and gun, which he kept in the car's compartment until needed. He knew his tanned face and arms betrayed the free moments he spent outdoors riding his sorrel mare.

"Detective Ryan Darnell. Glad to be of service," he responded in the same professional tone she had used. He could be as formal as any highbrow when it suited his purposes.

"And this is Scotty Tanner," she said, motioning the boy forward. "He reads lips and will be able to answer your questions if you look directly at him, speak slowly and evenly."

Since Ryan had grown up with an older cousin who had lost his hearing, her instructions were hardly necessary, but he nodded and did as she had instructed.

"Hello, Scotty."

A belligerent glare was all he got in return, making it quite clear what the boy's experience with the law must have been.

He's a tough one, all right, Ryan thought. He suspected the kid had created some kind of incident that had gotten out of hand and he was trying to cover it up with a bigger story. In any case, Ryan decided he wasn't going to waste time trying to get the initial information from him.

"Why don't you tell me what this is about, Miss Richards." He'd taken note that she wasn't wearing a wedding ring and guessed she must be in her thirties to have the position of director.

For a moment she worried her lower lip as if she wasn't quite sure where to begin. Then she said in a firm voice, "Scotty was not where he was supposed to be. I went looking for him. No one in the house had seen him so I checked the grounds and garage. I was heading for the small barn, when I saw him dashing into the stable. I hurried after him and found him hiding in the tack room. He was clearly shaken up." She paused and took a deep breath. "Apparently he had left the grounds. There's a small cabin on the property."

"I know where it is," he offered quickly. "About a half mile downstream." He'd even spent a night or two there on occasion in high school with some other guys when Alva's grandson, Stanley, had been living with his grandmother.

"Did Scotty break in? Is that what this is about?" Ryan suspected the boy swiped something out of the cabin and made up a story to cover his tracks.

"I didn't bring you way out here because of a little pilfering," she answered shortly. "I called you because Scotty said he saw a dead man lying on the floor in the front room."

"And you believe him?"

Her brown eyes snapped with impatience. "Yes, I do. Scotty was frightened because somebody else was there, too."

"Who?"

"He didn't see them but he felt the vibration of footsteps on the deck and ran." Her flashing eyes dared him to make light of the boy's story.

"All right. Let's take a look." He knew

nothing more would be gained by questioning either of them further. "We'll drive around to the cabin. It'll be quicker than hiking."

"I didn't know there was a road to the cabin."

"It goes a little ways past the mansion and then drops down to the cabin and the creek."

"Does Scotty have to go?" she asked, showing resistance to the idea. "I hate putting him through any more trauma."

"Finding out the real situation is the first priority, Miss Richards," Ryan countered flatly. He wasn't indifferent to the boy's feelings, but it couldn't be helped. If Scotty was making up the whole tale, he'd give himself away and put an end to this whole charade.

"You don't believe him about the body, do you?" she asked, fixing accusing honey-brown eyes on him.

"It's not my job to believe anything until I have evidence to support it," he replied evenly. "We need to verify how much, if any, of Scotty's story is true. But you don't have to go—"

"Yes, I do," she corrected curtly. "At the moment, I have to give this first priority." Turning to Scotty, she slowly mouthed the words telling him they were going for a ride in the car.

Swallowing hard, he asked in a wavering voice, "Am I going to jail?"

She shook her head and gave him a reassuring smile. "No. We just want to find out… who frightened you."

She put her arm around his shoulders, and they followed Ryan to the car. After guiding Scotty into the backseat, she quickly took her place beside him. Ryan closed the door behind them and there was a heavy silence in the car as he drove away from the mansion.

When he glanced in the rearview mirror, he could see worried lines on her forehead and he wondered what she was thinking. Marian Richards seemed too young and vulnerable to have the responsibility that went with a job like this one.

The nervous smile she gave Scotty seemed forced, and he'd bet anything she was really worried about being away from the mansion for any length of time. Hers must be a heavy responsibility. He hoped for her sake that this incident wasn't going to throw her job into any kind of crisis.

As the road mounted a slight incline, he could see the cabin below nestled in a drift of aspen trees near the stream. The place looked deserted, but it was evident that some of the encroaching undergrowth and over-hanging trees had been trimmed in order to keep the narrow road passable. Ryan decided to stop a short distance above the cabin so there wouldn't be any chance of disturbing any crime-scene evidence around it. He took out his shoulder holster and gun and put it on before getting out of the car.

"I want you two to stay here while I have a look around." Then he spoke slowly and directly to the boy. "How did you get in, Scotty?"

"I—I broke a window…in the back."

"And then?"

"I climbed in." The boy clenched his small fists as if ready to defend himself. "Then I got mad and trashed the kitchen."

"What do you mean trashed?"

"Knocked a bunch of stuff onto the floor."

"So you made a lot of noise?"

"I guess so."

"And nobody came?"

He shook his head.

"What did you do then?"

Scotty looked at Marian as if seeking re-assurance. She nodded and repeated, "What did you do then, Scotty?"

"I went into the other room."

"The one with the front door and large window?" Ryan prompted.

Scotty nodded. "And he was there."

"Who, Scotty?"

"The dead guy! On the floor! In front of the fireplace!" he yelled as if it was Ryan who was hard of hearing.

For the first time, Ryan believed Scotty was telling the truth. No pretense. No hint of lying. Nothing false about the boy's behavior. His eyes were rounded with honest fear.

"All right. Stay here. I'll check it out."

As Ryan quickly headed down the wooded slope to the log structure, his detective expertise immediately dictated his actions. He needed to verify if he was dealing with a crime scene and if so protect it from contamination. He slipped on his gloves as he approached the front door, which Scotty said had been locked.

He tried the doorknob in a way so as not to disturb any fingerprints. It was still locked.

Carefully making his way around to the back door, he searched for any signs of shoe prints on the deck but couldn't see any with the naked eye. Jagged shards of broken glass and an open window verified Scotty's entrance into the house, but when Ryan tried the back door it swung open easily.

The kitchen looked trashed, all right. Ryan tried not to touch anything as he carefully stepped past the clutter. He was treating everything about the cabin as a crime scene and drew his revolver when he reached the doorway of the living room, ready for any unexpected confrontation.

As his eyes surveyed the pleasant room filled with knotty-pine furniture, the only sound was the creaking of old timber settling in the log walls.

He slowly moved forward to a position in the room where he could see the fireplace. Since he was expecting to see a body lying there, he stared at the bare planked floor for a long minute in disbelief.

There wasn't any body! There wasn't any blood. There wasn't any sign that there had ever been a dead man lying there.

Chapter Three

When Marian saw Ryan coming up the slope toward them, she hurried forward to meet him. The glower on the detective's face wasn't reassuring.

"Did you find anything?"

"No," Ryan answered shortly. "I checked the whole cabin. No sign of a struggle. Nothing out of place except for a mess in the kitchen."

"Scotty told you he did that," she reminded him quickly.

"No sign of a body." He looked directly at Scotty. "Either there never was one or it has disappeared somehow."

Marian could tell from his tone which one of the two possibilities he believed. Remembering how terrified Scotty had been when she found him hiding, she was convinced the boy wasn't making up the story.

"Scotty's telling the truth," she said firmly. "He saw something or someone. And he felt vibrations of someone walking on the wooden deck."

"All right, we'll go with that for the moment. I'll take you two back to the mansion and alert our forensic crime-scene investigator to take a look. He'll tell us in quick order if there's any evidence in the cabin to support Scotty's story."

On the return trip to the mansion, Marian's thoughts were a mixture of frustration, apprehension and impatience. As she stared at the back of Ryan's handsome dark head, she wished she could be privy to the thoughts whirling there. Obviously, the detective had deep reservations about accepting Scotty's story at face value.

If she hadn't witnessed the boy's panicked fear herself, she might have suspected he was making up the story to divert attention from himself. She could handle a boyish prank, but what frightened her was the impact all this was going to have on her summer program if his terror was real.

"Will it be possible to keep this low-key? I mean, until your investigator takes a look at the cabin and knows something for sure?" she asked when they reached the mansion.

"Let's not cross any bridges yet. Toby Bower is one of the best and if he says we have a crime scene, it's out of my hands." He softened his tone. "He'll collect as much evidence as he can and take his findings back to the crime lab. Maybe he'll come up with something and maybe he won't. Until we know for sure, I'd advise you and Scotty to remain mum about what is going on."

She nodded in agreement, trying to keep the anxiety building inside from showing.

"I'm going back to the cabin now to wait for Toby."

"And you'll come back and tell me what he finds?" She knew her tone was more of a statement than a request, but she couldn't help it.

His mouth curved in a slight smile. "Yes, ma'am. I certainly will."

The way his dark blue eyes briefly locked with hers brought an unexpected warmth to her face. She quickly turned away, impatient with herself for reacting to his practiced charm. There wasn't a doubt in her mind that the good-looking detective could wind women around his little finger whenever it pleased him.

She watched him drive away and then

turned to Scotty. Putting her hands on his thin shoulders, she faced him squarely. "Don't tell anyone where we've been. Nobody. Understand?"

"I won't say nothing."

"Good."

As they came in the front door, the children were just trooping upstairs for a rest period. After telling Scotty to go upstairs with the others, she motioned to Rob, who was monitoring the group.

"Make sure Scotty stays resting on his bunk, Rob."

"What's the matter?" the teacher asked, raising an inquiring eyebrow. "Where'd you find him?"

"I'll tell you later," she lied and turned away before he could say anything more. She certainly was going to take the detective's advice and not share the unbelievable events of the afternoon with anyone. Just imagining what the fallout might be sent a nervous prickling up her spine.

She turned in a different direction and entered a small room next to the library that she'd chosen for her office. She groaned when she saw the telephone on her desk blinking, a stack of invoices still waiting on her desk for attention and information the Denver lawyer had requested ASAP still unanswered.

As disciplined as she usually was, she struggled to concentrate on catching up with her work. She couldn't help wondering what was happening at the cabin. What would the forensic detective find? Her stomach tightened with apprehension. How had a wonderful career opportunity suddenly become a threatening nightmare?

Could she trust the handsome Ryan Darnell? Even though he was obviously dedicated to doing everything by the book, he'd displayed a genuine concern for handling the situation as sensitively as possible. She appreciated that he hadn't put Scotty through an intense grilling. No doubt that would come later if the forensic investigation found anything relevant to the boy's story.

Marian knew that she was at a disadvantage not knowing how small-town police enforcement worked. She certainly hadn't expected to meet a well-built, nicely tanned man who looked like a handsome movie star assigned to play the part of a policeman. The way his cobalt-blue eyes could soften as he looked at her was totally unnerving. And what was worse, the gentle way he put his hands on Scotty made her own skin prickle.

She gave herself a mental shake. She was through with such foolishness. Her last romantic liaison had been several years ago and had ended with a pathetic whimper. Her total relief at being free again had been a warning that she didn't need a man to fulfill her life. She wasn't going to make the same mistake again no matter how many charming men like Ryan Darnell crossed her path.

RYAN WALKED TOWARD Toby's forensic van as the investigator parked behind Ryan's car. The small, energetic man in his forties had been in the Denver CSI office until a couple of years ago. He'd been born in New York City and had always worked out of a metropolitan coroner's office until he spent a vacation in Rock Creek and decided to settle in the small town as its only CSI investigator. Toby kept his light brown hair cut short and always wore a gray baseball hat and overalls when on duty.

Ryan admired the man's powers of observation, insatiable curiosity and dedication. "Thanks for coming right out, Toby."

"What do we have?" he asked, shifting a

carryall that contained all his portable forensic paraphernalia.

"Maybe we have a crime scene and maybe we don't."

"Sounds interesting."

Quickly, Ryan elaborated on the information he'd given Toby earlier on the phone. "My gut feeling is the boy is telling the truth, but I need you to verify it."

"Well, let's have a look," Toby responded with obvious interest as they walked down to the cabin.

Ryan stayed out of the way as Toby collected fingerprints from doorknobs, windowsills, and possible shoe prints on the deck and on the ground around the cabin.

Inside, Toby photographed the kitchen, front room, two small bedrooms and bathroom. He even took myriad photos of the wooden floors.

"Sometimes the camera picks up dust images that are not visible to the naked eye," Toby said as he carefully put the camera back in his carryall.

Ryan nodded in agreement. When he'd taken a couple of forensic classes at the Denver Police Academy, he'd found the work interesting, but had decided a crime laboratory wasn't the place he wanted to spend his days.

Toby shook his head when he'd finished doing everything that might offer a clue to what had really happened—if anything. "I really can't declare this a crime scene unless some evidence turns up to indicate there's been a felony of some kind."

"I know we can't launch a full investigation until we have something concrete," Ryan replied quickly. "But my concern is the boy may be in jeopardy while we're trying to establish if he really did witness a crime."

"Somebody could be intending to shut him up," Toby agreed. "Maybe you ought to keep him under surveillance for a few days. At least until I get the lab work done."

Ryan nodded. "Will you clear that with the chief?"

"I can try," Toby replied wryly. They both knew it would depend upon what kind of mood Police Chief Peterson was in when they made the request. "I don't think he'd want to leave the boy vulnerable to a possible killer."

"I don't think so either. I'll find an excuse for sticking around."

"I'm sure you will," Toby said with a

teasing smile. "Are there any good-looking women around?"

"One that I know of," Ryan admitted, but he wasn't all that sure the attractive Marian Richards would be happy about having an unexpected bodyguard underfoot. They'd have to find an acceptable reason for his presence for at least the next couple of days.

WHEN RYAN APPEARED in the office doorway, Marian's whole body stiffened.

"May I come in?" he asked politely.

"Yes, of course." She couldn't tell anything from his expression. Motioning to a nearby chair, she said, "Have a seat."

"Thanks, but I need to talk to Scotty. Where will I find him?"

His polite but official smile irritated her. She decided that if he wasn't intending to keep her informed, she'd better set him straight right now. "What more do you need to ask him?"

She wasn't prepared for his deep chuckle. "You're quite the guard dog, aren't you?"

"When I need to be."

He made a gesture of mock surrender. "Well, I guess you'd better come along then. I might need a witness in case I'm accused of child cruelty."

She knew he was teasing her, but she didn't care. Establishing her authority came natural to her. More than once she knew she had been referred to as Miss Ironsides.

"Rest period is just about ending," she said as she looked at her watch. "Scotty should still be on his bunk. I told our male teacher, Rob Harmon, to keep an eye on him."

"Good. Maybe Scotty's had time to remember a few more things."

As they made their way upstairs, she struggled with a growing impatience. What had the forensic examiner discovered? Why did Ryan want to question Scotty again?

A wave of children came pouring into the hall and down the stairs. An hour of outdoor activity was scheduled before dinner.

There were four bedrooms on both the second and third floors. Nancy and the nurse shared the large master suite on the second floor and two girls were assigned to each of the remaining three rooms. The same arrangement was made on the third floor for Rob and six boys. Marian knew they had to move quickly if they wanted to catch Scotty before he bolted down the stairs with the others.

She wondered if he'd gotten by them when the third floor echoed with emptiness as they walked by the vacant rooms. Her chest tightened when they reached the last one, but a wave of relief swept through her when they looked through the door and saw Scotty sitting on the edge of the top bunk, his legs dangling over the side.

Marian knew he'd picked this room because of the bunk bed. He'd made it clear that he didn't want "one of them sissy twin beds."

"Did you have a nice rest, Scotty?" she asked brightly when he sensed their presence and looked up. She knew the question was an inane one, but she was desperately trying to keep the moment as light as possible.

All color left Scotty's face as he glared at Ryan coming in behind her. He looked frightened, as if he expected the policeman to have a pair of handcuffs ready for him.

"Detective Darnell just wants to ask you a few more questions," she assured him.

Ryan held up two fingers as he stood in front of Scotty. "Two questions. Answer them and you can go outside and play games with the others. Okay?"

Scotty slowly nodded, a guarded look in his eyes.

"Did you see a car parked anywhere in the trees when you walked to the cabin?"

Scotty stared past Ryan's shoulder for a moment before he shook his head.

"Tell me, what did the dead man look like? Old? Young? His clothes? The color of his hair? Anything?"

Scotty sent Marian a frantic look, like someone backed into a corner. "I don't remember nothing."

She was ready to jump on Ryan for overloading the question, but he was already reassuring the boy. "If you remember anything later, Scotty, tell me. It could be important."

At that moment, Rob hurried into the room and seemed surprised to see Marian and Ryan there. "I've been busy getting things ready for a game of kick ball and came back to get him."

Scotty must have read the teacher's lips about kick ball, because he slid off the bunk and started toward the door.

"Is it all right?" Rob asked as he put a restraining hand on Scotty's arm.

Marian gave Ryan a questioning look.

"Great idea," he readily responded with a smile. "I think Scotty would love having a chance to kick something right about now."

After they were gone, Marian turned quickly to Ryan and demanded, "What did the forensic officer find?"

"Is there someplace we can talk privately?"

"My office—"

He shook his head. "Too many interruptions and we don't want anyone eavesdropping."

"Why all the need for privacy?" she asked, frowning. "If Rock Creek is anything like every other small town, the fact that a law officer was at the Wentworth estate will be tomorrow's gossip."

"True," he agreed. "But we can orchestrate the gossip to be what we want."

"How do we do that?"

"We put a spin on the truth," he said as he put a guiding hand on her arm as they walked down the hall to the stairs.

The only place Marian could think of that was off-limits to everyone was her own private quarters, which were on the ground floor near the solarium.

When Alva Wentworth's health began to decline, she had remodeled a spacious reception room and bathroom on the first floor into a parlor and a beautiful bedroom. A small refrigerator and hot plate sufficed for simple kitchen needs, and the buffet bar had remained intact. The wealthy widow had occupied these rooms the last few years before her declining health required an assisted-living facility.

"My rooms would probably be best," she told Ryan.

Under different circumstances, she certainly would have had second thoughts about inviting a man she'd met only a few hours earlier into her private suite, especially a physically attractive man who made her feel that she'd been missing vibrant male company for far too long.

Was she just imagining that when he put a guiding hand on her arm, his fingertips slightly caressed her soft flesh? She gave herself a mental shake as they made their way downstairs. Enough of such romantic nonsense!

She informed him in her director's voice, "I usually have a little time to myself during the activity period. We have the evening meal as soon as the children come in and I'll need to be in the dining room to help serve." She glanced at her watch. "We'll have about forty minutes. That should be enough time for you to bring me up to date."

If he was put off by her businesslike tone, he didn't show it. A half smile remained at the corners of his mouth as they made their way to another wing of the mansion. As Marian opened the door, the spaciousness of the former reception room still amazed her. Obviously Mrs. Wentworth had moved elegant cherrywood furniture from other areas in the house to furnish her private space. A beautiful sofa and chairs in burgundy velvet, graceful end tables and Tiffany lamps defined the sitting area, and a glimpse of the bedroom revealed a large canopy bed and antique furniture. These luxurious accommodations had been a special treat for Marian. She had deeply appreciated the fact that at the end of a long day, most of the clamor of staff and children was in the upper parts of the house.

Quickly she motioned Ryan toward one of the chairs and sat down opposite him on the sofa. She tried to keep her manner relaxed. "Now, then, what exactly did your investigator find that made you question Scotty again?"

"Nothing concrete. And that's the problem."

"I don't understand."

"Toby didn't find any blood anywhere, especially in front of the fireplace where Scotty said he saw the body. He looked the area over closely and took pictures. We'll have to wait to see if Toby got any fingerprints. No telling who's been using the cabin since Alva's been gone."

"The caretaker told me they hired a cleaning service for the mansion shortly before we took over. I don't know if the cabin was included in that or not. I could ask and find out."

"You are going to stay out of this," he said firmly. Leaning forward, his eyes locked with hers. "No one is going to know anything about what happened today."

"What do you mean?" She was startled by his tone and the sudden rigidity of his body.

"You haven't told Scotty's story to anyone, have you?"

"No."

"Good." He leaned back with obvious relief. "It's a pretty safe bet the boy hasn't said anything to anyone."

"I don't understand."

"You're not the only one," he admitted with a fleeting smile. "And that's the danger, Marian. Until we know if a crime has been committed, any talk and speculation could trigger something totally unexpected."

"But you just can't ignore—"

He quickly moved to the sofa beside her. "My first responsibility now is to keep Scotty and you safe. If someone did see the boy running away from a murder scene and knows the boy confided in you, both of you could be in danger." He put his hands lightly on her shoulders, turning her to face him. "Do you understand?"

"Are you trying to frighten me?"

"No," he replied in a softer tone. "I just intend to stay around and make sure neither of you are in jeopardy until we know exactly what we may be dealing with."

"I don't think that's possible. How can I explain your presence to everyone? You want me to lie about who you really are?"

"Not at all. We just have to put a little twist on the reason for me being here at the estate."

"Then you do mean lie."

"It's called a protective cover."

"And what could that be? It's hardly likely the staff will believe you're a volunteer staff member." Her mind raced ahead, already anticipating the problems of trying to incorporate a totally unlikely person into the curriculum.

"I was thinking more along the lines of something in keeping with the truth of my real occupation."

"And what would that something be?"

"How about your needing my services to check out or change the security system?"

"I could never do that without the permission of Arthur Kennedy. He's Alva Wentworth's Denver lawyer and controls the budget. We'd have to get his approval for such an expenditure."

"He's in Denver? How often does he show up here?"

"I never know," she admitted. "Most of the time we talk on the telephone. When he's in town, he reports everything personally to Alva and then gives me instructions. I have never made a move without their approval."

"Well, let's go with the security story as long as we can. That will give me a free hand to hang around and keep you and Scotty under protection."

"Do you think that's really necessary?"

"I don't know, but until we get something solid to go on, one way or the other, I intend to play it safe."

She could tell from the firmness in his voice it was useless to argue. In a way she felt relieved that he was taking charge. On the other hand, just thinking about him being a constant presence in her life created challenges on more levels than one. She was very aware of his physical warmth and sexual appeal. Having him around as a bodyguard night and day wasn't going to be that easy.

She rose abruptly to her feet.

"What's the matter?" he asked as he stood up beside her.

"The children will be coming in soon. I have to see to the dining room."

Something in her voice must have betrayed her anxiety, because he put his hands on her shoulders. "I'll make this as easy on you as I can. Just remember we're role-playing. Okay?"

"Okay," she echoed as firmly as she could.

"I'm here because you have been concerned for the security of the children and want me to check out the present system. I'll offer to remain on the premises until everything is brought up to date. Hopefully that will give Officer Bower time to carry out his forensic tests and provide us with some direction for any necessary investigation. I have a relative who is deaf and I can handle a little signing."

He fell silent as they walked through the house to the dining room.

"I need to check with Elsie Mullens, the cook," Marian said, turning toward swinging double doors leading into the kitchen. "We don't have any money in the budget for additional help, so all of us pitch in when we can. Two of the older children help load the two dishwashers and get a dollar a day for it. Scotty started out helping but gave Elsie such a bad time that she quickly decided to dispense with his services."

As they came into the kitchen, Elsie was filling bowls with a hearty vegetable soup. Platters of fried chicken, corn bread, fruit salad and peanut-butter cookies were side by side on the serving carts with pitchers of milk.

"Wow, everything smells delicious!" Ryan said enthusiastically as he smiled at Elsie. "I hope there's enough for one more."

"I wasn't told there was going to be a guest," she informed him in her blunt fashion.

"And I wasn't told there was a chef in the kitchen preparing good solid food that could send a man's stomach growling," he countered as he bent over and sniffed the vegetable soup. "Just a touch of oregano, I'll bet."

Elsie's frown instantly changed into an expression of surprise. "You some kind of a cook?"

"Nope, but I grew up on a ranch. We had

a chuck wagon cook who was a whiz at making a soup that smelled just like this."

"I've spent a lot of time during roundup cooking for a bunch of cowhands," Elsie said proudly as she gave him a full-blown smile.

"Really? I may just decide to stick around for a while. What do you think?" he asked as he turned to Marian.

"I guess you can take your time," she replied on cue. She was surprised how easily the lie flowed from her lips when she introduced Ryan to the cook. "He's going to be checking out the security system."

As Elsie wiped her hands on her apron, she scrutinized Marian's face and then Ryan's. Marian couldn't tell what was going through her mind but she knew the cook wasn't going to be easily fooled. If anyone saw through the charade they were creating, it would be Elsie. Once her suspicions were aroused, she could easily say or do something that could blow Ryan's undercover pretense sky-high.

Marian's mouth went dry.

And then what?

Chapter Four

When the children came in from their activity period, Marian went upstairs with Nancy to help the girls get ready for supper.

"All right, give," Nancy ordered, her round eyes sparkling with open curiosity. "Who is that hunk of masculinity in the kitchen? A parent checking us out?"

Marian shook her head. "No, his name is Ryan Darnell."

"And?" Nancy's full face spread in a teasing grin. "Do I detect something personal afoot?"

"Not at all. He's here on business." The lie came out easier than she thought it would. "He's checking out the security system."

"What's wrong with it?"

"Maybe nothing. That's what he's here to find out." In a way, that was the truth. If Scotty was lying, there wouldn't be anything to find out. Ryan Darnell would go back to his regular duties and this whole thing would be forgotten. She'd probably never have the occasion to see him again. And if he turned up something to verify Scotty's story, then…

She quickly shoved the thought away. The consequences were much too dire to even think about.

When Marian came into the elegant dining room with the rest of the teachers and children, she was surprised to find Ryan helping to set places at the one long table. She was amazed at the ease with which he handled water glasses, helped scoot in chairs and unfold napkins. Obviously, somewhere, sometime, he'd had plenty of practice.

Nancy winked at Marian as they walked to the end of the table where the adults sat, and whispered, "Let's jimmy the security system and keep him around."

Children as noisy as any in the hearing world took their places and began attacking the food and drink that had been put before them. A few of the youngsters had been finicky eaters when they first arrived, but they'd soon learned that meals were "eat up now or go hungry until the next one."

Henry Ziller, a tall, balding man in his

fifties, also showed up for the evening meal. His habitual scowl spoiled his appearance and he was the only one who ate without any interaction with kids or adults. Apparently he preferred Elsie's cooking to any he could do for himself in his small garage apartment.

For all intents and purposes, Henry ignored everything but the food. He'd made it quite clear to Marian that he felt Alva Wentworth had betrayed him by turning the place over to a bunch of do-gooders. He'd been in charge of the place for nearly twenty years. He was resentful, suspicious and obviously wanted them gone.

Marian watched Ryan ignore a chair at the adult end of the table and take one between Scotty and Mindy. When he signed something to the little girl, she laughed but Scotty just scowled and gave his attention to the food.

Marian's stomach tightened as the day's events played over in her mind. The detective was probably used to living on the edge of drama and trauma, but she prided herself on a well-ordered and uncomplicated life. How could events of just a few hours send her life into a tailspin?

When dinner was over, the children were taken into the large parlor for a movie before bed. Ryan remained behind in the empty dining room and so did Henry Ziller.

As the caretaker walked over to Ryan, his expression was like that of a guard dog ready to drive the intruder from the premises.

Apparently Ziller didn't remember him as one of the boys who had been at Stanley Wentworth's sleepovers in the cabin almost seventeen years ago. Ryan was not surprised and doubted if he would have recognized the caretaker if he'd met the balding, big-bellied, frowning man someplace else.

"You working here now?" Henry demanded bluntly. "Every time I turn around the old lady sends somebody else around to make my job harder."

Ryan had enough experience with hostile people to know that interviewing was about asking questions, not answering them. "You're the caretaker, aren't you?"

"Damn right! I see to the whole estate," he answered pugnaciously, as if ready for an argument.

"Oh, yes, Mr. Ziller. I remember you!" Ryan smiled as if the memory was a pleasant one. "You were the caretaker here the summer some of us high school kids were running around with Stanley Wentworth."

Obviously taken aback by this reference to the past, the caretaker deepened his scowl as Ryan stuck out his hand and forced a handshake. "Ryan Darnell. My folks have a place west of town."

"Don't remember you none," Henry replied flatly, still scowling. "Stanley's friends didn't mingle with the hired help. A snotty brat, he was. I'm glad the old lady cut him out of her will."

"I heard Stanley got himself into some kind of a jam and she disowned him." Ryan waited, hoping he might have turned on a valve that would bring him some personal information about the family.

Ziller only snorted.

Ryan let it go. The past was the past. He needed information about what was going on right now. Trying to butter up Ziller before asking him any specific questions, Ryan started with a compliment. "You've sure kept the place up fine, Mr. Ziller."

"And for what?" he snapped back. "Damn, if they haven't turned it into a camp for kids. The old lady let me run the place. Now they're ordering me around like I was some kind of flunky. You one of them teachers?" he demanded.

"No. I don't know who put in the request, but I'm to check out the security system around the place," Ryan answered smoothly. "We do that as a courtesy sometimes when the person is as respected as Alva Wentworth."

"There's not a damn thing wrong with our security." A flush of anger reddened Ziller's face. "Hell, I could have told you that. No need to make any changes. We've never—"

"Is the alert system a modern one?" Ryan interrupted smoothly. "Are all the doors hooked up to the main alarm? How about the windows? There must be three dozen in the whole place. Are they securely locked from the inside? And what about the garage, and other outbuildings?" Ryan deliberately omitted asking about the cabin. "Could anyone be prowling around the premises without being detected?"

"Nothing comes or goes without my knowing it!" Henry bellowed. "And that ain't about to change."

"Good. I'll put that in my report. Maybe we can make a few changes that will make your job easier. This place is a terrible responsibility for one man," Ryan said in a sympathetic tone.

"You're damn right it is!" Henry's glare softened slightly.

"Well, let's talk about it tomorrow," Ryan suggested.

"You staying here?"

"For a couple of days. I'll bunk upstairs with the boys. Maybe you can show me around the estate tomorrow when you have time?" Ryan made the request sound like a suggestion, but there was no consenting nod from Henry Ziller.

As Ryan turned away and walked out of the dining room, he could almost feel dagger eyes digging into his back. Clearly the caretaker didn't want anyone snooping around his domain. Ryan intended to find out why.

Pausing outside the open door of the living room, he peered in and saw that the children were watching a cartoon movie. Giggles and laughter verified that visual input was enough for hearing-impaired kids to enjoy the antics of Bugs Bunny.

He saw Scotty and Mindy sitting in the front row on some fold-down chairs. Nancy and Rob were positioned at the back of the room as if to make sure no one left without permission. As Ryan scanned the room, he didn't see any sign of Marian. Deciding she was probably in her office, he made his way to that wing of the mansion.

Light from the office was spilling out into the hall and he saw that she was just hanging up the phone as he came in.

"Don't you ever quit working?" he asked in a teasing tone.

When she looked up at him, he saw that her expression was akin to someone who had just been given some bad news.

"What's happening?" he asked bluntly as he walked over to her desk.

She moistened her lips and stared at him for a long minute. Then she stiffened her shoulders and said, "That was the Denver lawyer, Arthur Kennedy."

"And?" Ryan prompted when she hesitated to say anything more. She looked as if she was bracing herself against a destructive whirlwind.

"Kennedy called to say he's going to be here day after tomorrow for an update. There's no way I can pass you off as someone checking out the security system— not if I want to keep my position. Alva gave him power of attorney over everything connected with the estate and our program." She pushed back her chair and got to her feet. "It was understood when I was hired that I wasn't to make any kind of arbitrary decisions without the lawyer's permission. The man has already put me through the wringer over every decision I've made about our program."

"I can't believe he has the authority to fire you."

"Removed or replaced is the polite academic term," she corrected him grimly.

"That's not going to happen," he said firmly, stepping close to her. "You've done the responsible thing, calling the police. There may not be any need for pretense by the time he gets here. With any kind of evidence that a crime has been committed, I have the authority I need to take control. And if that happens, I doubt Mr. Kennedy would be inclined to dismiss you when you've acted wisely in the situation."

"I know how the big-city lawyer thinks. Keeping Scotty in the program won't be easy if he's guilty of orchestrating this whole thing."

Ryan had to resist putting his arms around her. He settled for lightly tipping her chin up so he could look straight into those soft brown eyes. "It's going to be all right."

She nodded but her eyes betrayed her fright, like those of a deer caught in the headlights of an oncoming car. He was startled by a suddenly overwhelming need to protect her at all costs. More than that he realized he wanted to draw her close and kiss those trembling lips. The sudden sexual attraction surprised him. His gaze must have dropped to her lips and revealed the focus of his thoughts. Instead of pulling away from his touch, her mouth seemed to part slightly with anticipation.

Then, she suddenly pulled back as a stampede of footsteps in the hall alerted them that the movie was over.

"I have to help get the children settled for the night."

The complete shift in the sexual ambience between them left him without words for the moment.

"I assume you want to bunk with Scotty?" she asked in a controlled voice that warned him not to pursue any emotions that might have been between them.

Following her professional tone, he replied, "Yes, if the boy decides to do any night roaming, I want to be his unseen shadow. And if he has any unexpected visitors, I want to be there."

"Surely he's safe enough inside the house," Marian asked with a worried look.

"That's why I'm here," he said. "I'll need to make a couple of calls and then I'll join him in his room. I guess the two boys are using the bunk, so I'll take the twin."

"Yes, that should work," she agreed. She hesitated as if she wanted to say something more, but turned toward the door as if deciding against it.

"Good night, then," he said, but she only gave him a quick nod as she left.

Glancing at his watch, he saw that it was just seven o'clock. Good. It was early enough to call his older sister, Ellen. He had found it handy that she lived in the same area as he did and had a key to his place.

Almost ten years older, Ellen had grown up mothering him and he rather liked it—most of the time. She was a registered nurse and seemed content with her own single status but was always after Ryan to find a woman and settle down.

Ryan picked up the desk phone and dialed her number.

"What's happening?" she asked when Ryan asked her to pack him a carryall bag.

"I'm not sure," he admitted. "I'm going to be at the Wentworth estate for a couple of days."

"The Wentworth estate?" she echoed. "What's going on?"

"Maybe nothing," he admitted. "I'll tell you all about it when I understand it myself. Could you run the bag out to me tonight? You know how to get here?"

"Of course. Everyone around Rock Creek knows where the exclusive Wentworth property is. Will I have any trouble driving up to the mansion?"

"No. Just don't miss the sign and turnoff from the main road." He described it for her. "Then follow the access road and it'll bring you right to the mansion."

"Okay, I'm on my way."

"Thanks, sis. I'll be waiting for you on the front steps. You're an angel."

"And don't you forget it," she teased as she hung up.

Ryan decided there was time to take a look at the front-door security system before he went out on the porch to wait for her. He might need to act knowingly about it.

It was as antiquated as he expected, and speculated that Alva must have put it in at least fifteen years ago. As far as he could tell, it was mainly a burglar alarm with no alert transfer to any kind of protective agency in case the security was breached.

Satisfied he'd chosen a good cover for his

presence in the house and on the grounds, he went out on the well-lighted veranda to wait for his sister. The beautiful summer evening was cool and pleasant with a soft, pine-scented wind flowing down from the nearby mountain slopes. Somewhere in the top of a tall ponderosa pine, a night bird was calling to the full moon.

As he stood there, leaning against one of the pillars, his thoughts turned unwittingly to the desirable woman he'd almost kissed. She had been willing, he was positive. He'd recognized a longing in the depths of those golden-brown eyes and he'd felt a response shoot through his own body. Never before had he even been tempted to indulge in momentary pleasures when he was on the job.

When he saw a pair of headlights coming through the drift of trees along the mansion's driveway, he straightened and walked down the front steps.

His sister had made good time, he thought, but as the car came nearer, he realized it wasn't his sister's secondhand sedan.

"What in the…" He swore as he recognized the late-model sports car immediately. It belonged to Joyce Phillips, a former girl-friend and his fiancée until a couple of years ago. Their romance had been a high school infatuation that had slowly turned into something more for a brief time.

When Ryan left to attend the police academy in Denver, they had parted ways. Joyce had stayed in town and become a hairstylist in a local beauty shop, and was there to greet him when he came back to Rock Creek to stay. She was still the same vivacious, outgoing woman who had been a cheerleader and prom queen, but the adolescent attraction Ryan had felt for her was gone. As far as Joyce was concerned, she'd made it clear that she was just waiting for Ryan to come to his senses and marry her. Unfortunately a lot of people like his sister were still doing their best to get them back together. It was just like Ellen to send Joyce on the errand instead of coming herself.

Joyce was petite, with a round face framed by short, dyed-blond, curly hair. She still had the sexy kind of figure that looked great in short cutoffs, tank tops and hip-hugging jeans. Sometimes he couldn't believe his own reluctance. *What in blazes was he waiting for?*

"Hi, handsome," she greeted him. "Delivery service."

He smiled as he met her at the bottom of

the stairs. "I appreciate it, Joyce, but you shouldn't let my sister con you like that."

"It was my idea, really," she admitted as her eyes roved over the front of the mansion. "I couldn't pass up this chance to get a real close look." Then she added pointedly, "I'm dying to see the inside."

Now he remembered once again why being with Joyce was so wearing. She seldom took in the reality of any situation. Somehow she expected everything to be within the bounds of her desires.

"I'm afraid that won't be possible," he said firmly.

"Why not?" Her tone registered total disappointment at not getting her way. "Your sister told me you were going to be here a couple of days. Why can't you show me around?"

"I'm on duty."

"What kind of duty?"

"Police work. That's what I do. Remember?"

"Oh, I remember," she answered, frowning. "Honey, that's been the problem all along, hasn't it?"

"Maybe, and it's not going to change, Joyce," he said.

"I guess not." Sighing, she moved closer to him. "Even when you feel this way about me."

Before he could move back, she threw her arms around his neck and kissed him with moist open lips.

As adolescents, she had paved his way to manhood with all kinds of lustful experiences. For an instant, remembered passion betrayed him and dulled his senses to anything but an automatic response.

Then he jerked back and said in a low voice, "Joyce, go back to town and tell Ellen her little scheme didn't work."

Picking up his bag, he turned toward the front steps and that's when he saw Marian standing in the front doorway, then turning and rushing away. Damn.

She'd probably seen Joyce's little demonstration and gotten the wrong idea. He didn't know why it should matter. But it did.

He was debating about hurrying to catch up with her and explain the situation with Joyce, when his inner sensible voice asked, *What makes you think she'd even care?*

Chapter Five

Marian turned restless in bed, her emotions much too muddled to think clearly. A kaleidoscope of the day's events kept her body tense and her mind racing. She couldn't be sure the deception Ryan had proposed wouldn't jeopardize her position. She would be held accountable for whatever happened. Ryan's true identity was bound to come out at some point and their lies would be exposed. Why had she listened to him? Her confidence in Detective Ryan had wavered.

Why? Because you saw him kissing a young woman good-night? She immediately rejected such an absurd idea. She barely knew the man. One thing was sure, he knew how to turn on the sexual charm. Remembering the way he had gently touched her face and caressed her with his eyes, she blushed to think how readily she'd wanted him to kiss her. She couldn't believe how she had responded to his unexpected advances. Well, he wouldn't catch her off guard again. She'd learned the hard way through a couple of unfortunate romances that a competent, ambitious woman was a threat to any man she might want in her life. Thank heavens for the interruption that kept her from making a fool of herself.

She turned over and pounded her pillow. That little good-night scene she'd witnessed had knocked some sense into her. Hearing voices, she had gone to the door. Then she'd been startled and embarrassed that he might think she was spying on him. Turning quickly away from the front door, she had hurried to her room and shut the door. When the minutes passed without any sign of him, she assumed he had gone directly upstairs to bed. In a way she was relieved. She needed time to think and examine her own feelings. She shouldn't have been surprised that a man as attractive and sexy as Detective Ryan Darnell had a woman waiting in the wings to kiss him good-night. One thing was sure, he certainly possessed a subtle male magnetism that must provide him with plenty of female companionship.

She jerked her thoughts away from this kind of speculation. His private life was not her concern. What worried her was the deception he had proposed as his cover.

Lying and keeping silent about the real reason she had called in the authorities might not be in her best interest. Should she wait until the forensic reports were in before confiding in her superiors about the true situation? And what about Scotty? Would she be forced to dismiss him from the program because of his truancy? If her silence would protect him, how could she put his future in jeopardy by speaking out before they knew the real situation? What would happen when Arthur Kennedy arrived?

After a fitful sleep, she slipped out of bed when the nightstand clock showed it was five-thirty. After showering, she quickly dressed in a pair of black jeans, a white knit top that hugged her waist and hips, and hurriedly tied the laces on her walking shoes. She vigorously brushed her shoulder-length hair, leaving her bangs and a few wisps of curly strands to frame her face. The heavy-lidded eyes that looked back at her from the mirror hinted at her sleepless night.

"You'll look better after a cup of Elsie's

strong coffee," she told herself as she headed out the door.

A large grandfather clock in the main hall was just chiming six o'clock when she made her way to the kitchen.

Elsie was already busy preparing breakfast. "What are you doing up so early?" she asked Marian in her usual gruff way.

"Couldn't sleep," Marian replied honestly.

The cook lifted an inquiring bushy eyebrow as she gave Marian a half smile. "What's the matter? No sweet dreams?"

"Not one."

"You could have fooled me. Anyone with eyes in his head could tell something was going on between you and that Ryan fellow."

"Strictly business."

"Yeah, sure. I noticed he's not wearing a wedding ring. Is he going to be sticking around for a spell?" she asked as she drew a pan of biscuits out of the oven.

"I'm not sure, but I hope not."

Elsie set down the pan and turned to Marian. "I don't understand why a good-looking gal like you would prefer to be an old maid than go after a dream like him."

"That's the problem."

"What is?"

"Sometimes dreams turn into nightmares."

"Hmm, I guess. I'm ignorant about what is dream material these days. When I was your age, a tall, wide-shouldered fellow with a firm jaw and deep blue eyes would have filled the bill. What kind of a guy are you waiting for?"

"I'm not sure," she admitted with a feeble smile.

Elsie shrugged and handed Marian a box of oatmeal. "Make yourself useful."

The children were beginning to clomp down the stairs and make their way to the dining room, when Ryan unexpectedly appeared in the kitchen doorway.

"Need some extra help?"

"Always." Elsie gave him a wide smile and handed him a tray of glasses filled with orange juice. As her eyes passed over his tight jeans and the snug T-shirt molding his chest and shoulders, she nodded approvingly.

If he was surprised to see Marian there, wearing an apron and dishing up oatmeal, he didn't show it. Did he assume a woman's place was in the kitchen? she wondered.

"You're an early riser," he said as he gave her one of those engaging smiles of his.

"Sometimes."

"And early to bed?" This time the inflection was questioning. Had he seen her in the doorway and known she was avoiding him when he came in?

"Sometimes," she repeated in the same casual tone. She wasn't about to admit he'd been in her thoughts most of the night. She pretended to concentrate on filling the cereal bowls.

They exchanged only a half-dozen words while working in the kitchen. Was he puzzled by the distant way she was behaving toward him? Did he suspect she'd changed her mind about deceiving everyone about his true identity?

When they had finished bringing all the food into the dining room, she sat in her usual place at the table and Ryan took the chair between Scotty and Mindy as he had the night before. He divided his attention between the two children and both of them seemed to respond to his friendliness. Scotty almost even laughed a couple of times at Ryan when he tried to sign something.

Several times he glanced at Marian during the meal, his expression one of frowning speculation, as if he was aware of the distance her behavior was putting between them.

She wanted to make him understand the

reason for not wanting to go along with his deception. No doubt, he was used to using undercover techniques in his police work and he seemed to be proceeding according to some kind of accepted investigation agenda. That was well and good for an officer of the law, but she was in a very vulnerable position. If a crime had been committed on the premises, lying about it to her superiors, even for a couple of days, could send her packing. No job. No recommendation. No upward career.

If there had been a crime?

After the children had finished eating, they bounded out of the room with Rob, Nancy and Bertha in their wake. Marian stayed to put the staff's dirty dishes on a serving cart.

Ryan walked over to her and before she could tell him she wanted to clarify some things with him, he began asking her questions about Henry Ziller.

"Doesn't the caretaker have breakfast with everyone?"

"No. He keeps to himself except for the evening meal."

"What about the rest of the day? Is he in and out of the house?"

"I suppose so. I really haven't noticed. I've

been busy with other things," she added almost defensively. Didn't he realize that she had her hands full supervising students and staff? The caretaker's schedule was not her concern. Henry had been Alva Wentworth's employee for years. Someone told her she'd hired him right after he got out of the army as a young man.

"Do you know if he leaves the premises on any regular basis?"

"I have no idea. Elsie would be more able to answer your questions. She pretty much knows what's going on with everybody." Marian refrained from telling Ryan that he was at the top of the cook's curiosity list at the moment. If anyone figured out the detective wasn't really here to check the security system, it probably would be Elsie.

"Okay, I'll check with her. I don't suppose you have any kind of personal file on Ziller?"

"No, why are you asking about him?"

He softened his tone. "It's my job to ask about everyone. I know this can't be easy for you, Marian."

"You're right, it isn't," she replied with spirit. "I'm not comfortable one bit with holding back the truth."

"Not even if Scotty's safety is the reason?"

The question took her by surprise. "What do you mean?"

"Timing can be everything in a case like this," he explained patiently. "If Scotty is lying, withholding punishment for a couple of days isn't going to hurt anything. If the boy is telling the truth and there's been a murder connected somehow to the estate, it's important that I do some groundwork while we're waiting for Toby's report."

She wanted to argue that everything should be put out on the table now. Waiting seemed to just be a cover-up that could backfire. Still, the precariousness of her future suddenly seemed inconsequential when viewed from his perspective.

"All right. We'll play it your way."

"Good. I'll try to work around the children's schedule as I do my investigation. What's happening this morning?"

"Study time with teachers until midmorning. Games outside until noon. Then Elsie is planning an outdoor lunch, and we'll take the children down to a grassy area by the stream and have a picnic."

"Scotty will be under the supervision of the teachers until then?" he asked.

"Yes, that should give you some time this

morning to…to…" she stammered. "To check the security system."

Leaning close to her ear, he whispered, "Lying comes easier with practice."

As she felt the warmth of his breath on her cheek and drew in the spicy smell of his aftershave, her senses reeled with his closeness. The truth of his words were bittersweet. How truthful was he being with her about the investigation and anything else? No doubt he would provide a glib reason for having a woman come by for a good-night kiss. She was determined not to let her emotions dictate a lack of judgment where the detective was concerned.

"I'll be in my office for an hour, until recreation period. I usually help out with some of the games. Rob takes the older kids for a game of baseball. Nancy and I handle the younger ones."

"Good, I'll join you. In the meantime, I'll pay Ziller a visit and have a little chat with him."

AS RYAN HEADED for the garage apartment, he tried to figure out exactly what was going on with Marian. Her reservation about being a part of his deception was understandable, but her sudden coolness implied something more. He knew she'd seen Joyce kissing him, but whether or not he had a girlfriend, past or present, was personal business. His first priority was to determine if a felony had been committed and if Scotty was in danger. He could not let his feelings or hers be an issue in the situation.

Last evening, he'd parked his car in the only vacant spot in the garage, but as he walked past the open door, he noticed there was an empty space this morning and something else that hadn't been there before. A dirty, gray motorcycle was parked against one wall and he wondered if it belonged to the caretaker.

Ryan quickly mounted the outside wooden staircase, knocked firmly on the door and bent his ear closer to hear any movement. A muffled sound told him someone was inside.

He was startled when the door suddenly jerked open and he faced a scowling young man who was short and stocky, wearing faded jeans and a cotton shirt that wasn't tucked in. Ryan guessed him to be in his late teens or early twenties.

"Oh, hi, I am looking for Mr. Ziller," Ryan said quickly, masking his surprise.

"Ain't here," he snapped, peering at Ryan through strands of uncombed brownish hair in need of a good shampoo.

"Oh?" Ryan raised an eyebrow in mock surprise. "We were supposed to check out the security system."

"Don't know nothing about that," he retorted and started to close the door.

Ryan moved quickly forward into the room.

"I told you he ain't here!"

"Well, I guess I could wait a bit for him." Ryan glanced over at the small kitchen at one end of the room. No sign of a coffeepot or dirty dishes. "He didn't come to the house for breakfast," Ryan commented. "Did he eat here?"

"I was still asleep when he left. And if he went to town, no telling when he'll be back."

"I didn't know Henry had a helper. Maybe you could show me around? What's your name?"

"Victor Blaise. And I ain't no helper," he snapped. "I'm Henry's nephew."

"Oh, nice to meet you, Victor. And you live here with him?"

"Hell, no," he swore. "I just rode over on my bike for a short spell."

"Oh, where are you from?"

"I don't stay anyplace long."

I bet you don't, thought Ryan. He'd also bet the purpose of Victor's visits was to put a touch on his uncle for money. "How long have you been here?"

"Too damn long. Nearly a week."

"Well, it's a nice place to relax. Do a little fishing and hiking. Have you taken any walks around the estate?"

"No," he replied quickly. "My uncle don't like me wandering around." His defensive tone made it pretty clear he'd been doing exactly that. Ryan added Victor to the list of people who had been on the premises yesterday, if and when a crime occurred.

"There are kids all over the place," Ryan commented in a complaining tone. "I suppose you've seen them running around?"

"Yeah. My uncle says the old woman has lost her marbles. He's ready to throttle the whole pack of them."

For the next few minutes, Ryan tried to keep the conversation going, hoping to find out as much about the caretaker as he could, but Victor clammed up.

Finally, Ryan decided he'd probably get more information from Elsie, as Marian suggested. "Tell your uncle I was looking for him," Ryan said as he started to leave.

Victor gave an impolite grunt in reply.

Ryan was willing to bet the message never got delivered.

Elsie was busy preparing the picnic lunch when he came into the house. She already had a pile of sandwiches bagged and was preparing cookie dough to bake.

"I was looking for Ziller," Ryan said as he helped himself to a cup of coffee and sat down on a high stool close to where she was working. "I talked to his nephew but he didn't seem to know where he was."

Elsie rolled her eyes to the ceiling. "That one wouldn't know it was raining if he was drowning in it."

"Not too bright, huh?"

"The worst kind!"

"Why do you say that?"

"I guess Victor's been in all kinds of trouble. Just stupid stuff, mostly, from what Henry says. He gives him money because he promised his dead sister that he'd try to look after him."

"Have you seen Victor wandering around the place?" Ryan asked casually.

"Nope, but I don't stick my head out of this kitchen very often. Picnic lunches are a lot of work but I love being outside. Did I tell you I was a chuck wagon cook on a ranch?"

Ryan nodded and she was off and running down memory lane, telling him amusing stories about herself and all the cowhands that had come around to compliment her on her cooking.

When study period was over and Ryan heard the bustle of children running outside, he excused himself after promising Elsie to help take the picnic lunch down to the creek.

Scotty was one of the first boys out of the house and seemed startled to find Ryan waiting for him. He hung back as some of the older boys brought out the balls and bats and Rob followed with some flat stone markers for bases.

"Would you like Scotty and me to set those out for you?" Ryan volunteered. He could tell the way Scotty was acting that he was an outsider, not one of the group.

"Sure, great! The field doesn't have to be regulation," he told Ryan with a slight wink.

As Ryan and Scotty marked off the field, Marian came out of the house with Nancy and the girls. They moved a safe distance from the boys' baseball field and set up a small portable net for a game of volleyball. The activity hour passed quickly. Ryan was pleased when Scotty hit a home run.

When everyone started walking across the meadow toward the stream, Rob asked Ryan if he and Scotty would take the croquet set and put it in the picnic area.

Scotty looked less than happy when Ryan nodded and Rob handed him the wire wickets.

While the food was being set out on the picnic tables and blankets spread around on the ground for sitting, the children wandered along the creek bed. Some of the boys began throwing rocks into the water and others floated sticks like boats in the swiftly moving, white-foamed water.

"No, you can't wade," Nancy said and signed firmly when a couple of the little girls took off their shoes.

Ryan and Scotty were putting the wickets in the ground, when suddenly a child's scream brought the eyes of those who could hear to the creek. The rest soon followed when they learned what had happened.

"Amy's in the water!" someone shrieked.

Ryan bolted down to the water's edge and plunged into the waist-high swirling water. The little redheaded girl had tried to walk across a fallen log and had lost her footing. She'd tumbled into the stream and was slowly losing her grip on one of the dead branches.

Ryan grabbed her just as a rushing current started to take her downstream. Lifting her in his arms, he carried her out of the water. He knew well how treacherous a mountain stream could be, flowing swiftly over boulders and falling into deep holes. Thank heavens, he'd been close enough to catch her before the current swept her away.

As he laid the little girl on the ground, she was gagging and gasping. He quickly turned her into the correct first-aid position to help empty her lungs, thankful his paramedic's training had come in handy more than once.

"Get the nurse. Get the nurse!" someone yelled.

By the time Bertha got there, the child had stopped gagging and had begun breathing more normally. She was even sitting up when the nurse checked her vital signs.

Marian had remained sitting on the ground beside the little girl. She had been the first one by Ryan's side as he worked on the little girl. When he heard Marian's deep sigh of relief that the child had just suffered a good ducking, he was aware of the heavy responsibility on her slender shoulders for the welfare of all these hearing-impaired youngsters.

After a few minutes, the drenched child was herself again. Marian hugged her, murmuring, "It's all right, Amy. It's all right."

The little girl didn't hear the words, but she knew what the hug meant. "I go swimming."

Everyone laughed.

Bertha helped Amy to her feet and signed, "Next time wear a bathing suit. You're soaking wet. Let's go get some dry clothes."

As the crowd broke up and headed back to the picnic area, Ryan was surprised when Marian looked up at him with tears edging the corners of her eyes. "Thank you."

He started to say something light and airy, but the words never came out. There was something wordless about the way they looked at each other, and when they heard Elsie's cowbell and her bawdy "Come and get it," they walked slowly back to the picnic area without speaking, motioning the children to follow.

A line of eager youngsters was already forming in front of a picnic table loaded with food. Ryan expected to see Scotty at the front, his plate held out for everything Elsie had prepared. As he searched for a blond unruly head of hair, there was no sign of the boy anywhere near the picnic area.

Thinking that he might be finishing the job of setting up the croquet set, Ryan quickly walked over to that area. Everything was still on the ground the way they had tossed it when Ryan heard Amy's cry for help.

He glanced at his watch. He couldn't believe it. That had been nearly forty minutes ago. Had Scotty been in the crowd watching the rescue? One thing was sure, he wasn't anywhere in the picnic crowd.

When Ryan asked Rob if he had seen Scotty go to the house with some of the athletic equipment while they were waiting on the food, the teacher shook his head.

"I told him where to pile it and said we'd take it up later. I intended to keep him busy with a couple of other chores but forgot it with the near drowning. Has he taken off again?"

"I'm not sure."

"I warned him to obey the rules," Rob said, frowning. "I told him he didn't have any free throws left as far as I was concerned."

Just what the kid needed, Ryan thought with a rush of fear. He would have thought that Rob would have realized Scotty needed a friend in the bull pen.

He wanted to make sure Nancy and Elsie hadn't sent him on an errand.

"Haven't seen him," Nancy replied, looking around as she spoke. "Did he run off again?"

Elsie frowned. "I haven't seen him in the chow line and I would have expected him to go through at least twice by this time."

When Ryan spied Mindy sitting on the ground with her picnic plate and a glass of lemonade, he knelt down beside her and carefully mouthed, "Scotty? Where is Scotty?"

She put down her fork and then pointed in the direction of the house.

He gave her shoulder an affectionate squeeze. Then he quickly headed across the open meadow to the back door of the mansion. He was hoping he might find Scotty in the kitchen, playing the loner and snatching his own lunch from the refrigerator or cupboard.

No such luck. The kitchen appeared to be pretty much the way Elsie would have left it.

He headed for the stairs, and took them two at a time as he went up to the third floor. Once again, he hoped to find Scotty, probably stretched out on his bunk in a belligerent mood.

The room was empty and there was no

sign that Scotty had been back since he left that morning.

Ryan's irritation slowly edged toward something akin to apprehension. Had Scotty left on his own? Where would he go? Was the boy fearful enough to try to find his own hiding place…without food, money or help?

Another scenario quickly formed in Ryan's mind. If Scotty hadn't run on his own, could someone have enticed him away while everyone had rushed to watch the near drowning?

Hurriedly he made his way back downstairs, mentally organizing an immediate search of the area. He had just about reached the kitchen again, when he heard something that sounded like glass shattering.

Maybe Scotty had been hiding from him. Relieved, he hurried into the kitchen, but his relief was short-lived.

It wasn't Scotty who had dropped a glass of milk on Elsie's clean floor, but Victor, the caretaker's nephew.

"I was just… I thought I'd help myself," he said.

Ryan cut off his defensive rambling with a wave of his hand. "I'm looking for a blond-headed boy, eleven years old. Have you seen him?"

Instantly Victor's mouth relaxed. Obviously pleased, he asked, "Is he in some kind of trouble?"

Ryan shoved Victor back against the refrigerator. "Have you seen him?" Ryan demanded.

Victor swallowed hard and nodded.

"Where is he?"

"I—I don't know," he stammered.

"Where'd you last see him?"

"Coming out of the garage."

"When?"

"A while ago. The kid was riding a bicycle and heading down the front road as fast as he could pedal."

Chapter Six

Ryan immediately called the police station and told the dispatcher, "I need an all points bulletin put out for a boy named Scotty Tanner. He's eleven years old, hearing-impaired, slender build, longish blond hair and blue eyes. He's wearing faded jeans and a white T-shirt. He left the Wentworth estate riding a red bicycle. I'm pretty sure he's heading into town or is already in the city limits. Let me know if you pick him up, and detain him until I get there."

"We're on it," she replied promptly.

As he hurriedly left the house and headed for the garage to get his car, Marian caught up with him.

"What's happening?" She was out of breath from running to overtake him.

A few minutes ago she'd finished serving lunch and helped all the children get settled on their picnic blanket. Then she'd looked around for Ryan and Scotty, hoping maybe the three of them could eat together.

Where were they? She knew they'd been helping Rob with the croquet set. When she asked if he knew where they were, Rob had shaken his head. "I guess Scotty took off and Ryan is looking for him."

"When did he leave?" she asked, trying to keep the sudden apprehension out of her voice.

"I guess when all of us were paying attention to Amy. Anyway, Ryan headed for the house to try to find him."

"Thanks, I'll check it out."

Before she reached the house, Ryan came out alone and headed toward the garage. She could tell from his tight expression that something was wrong.

"Where's Scotty?"

"Apparently he took off on a bicycle."

"When?"

"Most likely while everybody's attention was on Amy's rescue. My guess is that he's already made the five miles into town by now. I'm heading out to look for him."

"I'm going with you," she declared as Bertha and Amy came out of the house at that same moment, heading back to the picnic.

In the past the nurse had filled in when necessity took Marian away from the estate, and the staff and children accepted her authority without argument.

Marian called to Bertha, "I have to leave. Take charge until I get back."

"Will do," she answered with a wave of her hand.

Marian tried to keep step with Ryan's long stride and ask him questions at the same time.

"How did you find out he left on a bicycle?"

"Ziller's nephew saw him leave."

"There are some old bikes stored in the garage. I've been thinking about getting them in shape for the kids to ride." She worried her lip. "I guess I should have seen to it that they were locked up. I never thought—"

"Of course you didn't," he said as they reached the garage and hurriedly got in his car. "And I should have kept a tighter leash on the kid."

"And let Amy drown?" she retorted.

As they drove away from the estate, she leaned forward in her seat as much as the seat belt would allow. Her eyes searched the area along the road on both sides. Maybe he had pulled off to rest or explore. Maybe they would find him before they reached the main road into town.

When she expressed this hope to Ryan, his expression remained unchanged, with his lips set in a firm line and eyes narrowed in concentration.

"My bet is he's already reached Rock Creek's city limits," he replied. "Scotty is a city kid and will know how to lose himself. He may be damn hard to find." He shot her a quick glance. "You all right?"

"Fine," she lied.

As they traveled down the main road to town, the traffic increased. Ryan swore as they were hemmed in by a slow line of cars heading into town.

"Blast it all. I forgot that this is the day Rock Creek begins its annual celebration of Pioneer Days. People from this area and some from as far away as Colorado Springs gather to enjoy parades, carnival and the rodeo at the county fairgrounds. Traffic in town is always horrendous," he said as he slapped an agitated hand on the steering wheel. "There'll be boys all over town riding bikes."

"The town's not that big," she protested. "Surely you have an adequate police force to handle a missing child."

"Under ordinary circumstances. The

town's population will increase tenfold this week. The streets will be packed. Motels and hotels full. Roadside parks filled with campers and picnics."

"How do we know he headed in the direction of town and not north?"

"We don't, but it's all uphill north. Scotty would be familiar with the road into town because that's the way the bus brought him to the estate."

When the slow-moving traffic into town came to a dead stop, Ryan's explosive impatience made it clear to Marian that finding Scotty was more than just a routine assignment to him. She'd had enough counseling experience to recognize he was acting like a family member concerned for a lost child. He had bonded with Scotty on an emotional level and somehow that made it easier to handle her own frustration.

Any runaway child under her supervision would have rocked her to the core, but the circumstances surrounding Scotty's disappearance were devastating. She kept asking herself what she should have done differently. How had it happened that a boyish rebellion was mushrooming into an unbelievable nightmare?

She'd spun a web of lies around Ryan

Darnell's presence at the estate, allowing him to take charge of Scotty. Now she felt she'd neglected her own responsibilities by not watching the boy herself, and wondered how she could possibly explain all of this to the foundation that had hired her.

When the traffic started moving again, Marian kept her eyes fixed on the passing landscape for a glimpse of a blond-headed kid resting his bike at the edge of a wooded area.

"Thank God," breathed Ryan when the line of traffic began to move and a short time later dissipate in different directions at the edge of town.

Instead of continuing toward town, he abruptly turned onto a state highway heading away from Rock Creek.

"Why are we going in this direction?" Marian demanded immediately.

"The local cops will be handling the downtown area," he explained. "The state highway patrol has been notified of our all points bulletin and their units are spread over a greater area. It seems more likely to me that a frightened boy would try to make time on his bike and get away from everybody as quickly as he could. I think Scotty would take off down the highway."

"But how far would he go? The next town is at least twenty miles away, isn't it? He'd have to stop somewhere to rest."

"I agree. And he'll undoubtedly need to get water at some point. There's a truck stop just down the road. Let's see if anybody there has seen him."

There were at least a dozen cars and half that many trucks in the parking lot of the combined gas station and café. No sign of any bicycles, red or otherwise, parked outside.

As they went into the café, Ryan gave her some quick instructions. "Start down the line of booths and ask if anyone has seen a blond young boy riding a red bicycle."

She nodded. It felt good to be doing something.

"I'll check the counter and tables." He surprised her by giving her a fleeting grin as he added, "And don't worry. We'll find him."

All she could do was give a small smile in return and nod her head before walking away. She'd never met a man who put her emotions in such a tangle.

It only took them ten minutes to canvas the truck stop. No luck.

Even though they hadn't eaten lunch,

neither had an appetite and they left as quickly as they could.

"There's a pullout rest stop about a mile up the road," Ryan said when they were back in the car. "It has restrooms, a drinking fountain and picnic tables under the trees. Maybe we'll have better luck there."

"I don't think he could have made it that far," Marian protested, still having the feeling they should be looking in town for him.

"Well, let's check. We can always turn back."

As they left the highway and parked in front of a low brick building, they could see several groups of people enjoying the picnic area.

"If Scotty got this far, he'd be hot, hungry and thirsty," Ryan said as they got out of the car. "He might try to bum lunch from somebody."

Ryan headed toward one of the outdoor grills where a couple of men were serving up hot dogs and hamburgers, and Marian turned in the opposite direction. She passed a couple sitting in lawn chairs, eating while two dogs were leashed to nearby trees. They barked so loudly Marian had trouble hearing their answer.

"No, we haven't seen a deaf boy on a bicycle."

She got the same answer two more times

before she suddenly froze when she glimpsed a boy, Scotty's size, wearing a baseball hat and sitting under a nearby tree.

Her heart began to race as she moved closer.

"Scotty?" she asked as she tapped his head gently.

As he looked up at her, Marian's heart sank with disappointment. His hair was darker and his boyish face was round, freckled, with a sunburn peeling on his nose.

"Sorry. I thought you were someone I knew," Marian said as he looked at her with a puzzled expression. "I'm looking for a boy about your age pedaling a red bicycle. Have you seen him anywhere around?"

"Nope. It's too hot for bike riding," he replied flatly as he took another bite of the chicken leg he held in his hand. "But a great day for a picnic."

"Yes, isn't it?" Marian said with a catch in her throat, thinking about the lunch Elsie had prepared. Why hadn't she realized Scotty was frightened enough to run away? Wherever he was, he must be tired, hot and hungry by now. And very scared.

She was returning to the car in defeat, when she saw Ryan coming toward her at a quickened pace. He was talking on his cell phone and his alert expression suddenly sent a quiver of hope through her.

As he hung up and shoved the phone in his pocket, he told her with a broad smile, "A city cop picked him up, red bicycle and all!"

Relief sluiced through her with a force that made her knees weak. She felt like laughing and crying at the same time.

Ryan reached out and cupped her elbow. "Steady now. Come on, let's go to the station and claim him."

Congested traffic made the return trip to town an exasperating snail-paced crawl. Not only were cars, buses and pedestrians clogging the streets, but horseback riders heading for the fairgrounds kept their mounts clopping along at a leisurely pace.

"Where did they find him?" Marian asked, trying to still her happy nervousness.

"In the downtown district. I guess I was wrong about him heading into town. An officer nailed him as he tried to take off again on the bicycle. He wouldn't tell him his name."

Marian wasn't surprised. She'd never seen anyone his age who could defy the whole world.

The police station was a brick building set

two blocks past the courthouse. A nearby park was crowded with school-band members who were having a picnic after marching in the parade. Marian realized it was something of a miracle that Scotty had been noticed at all in the holiday bedlam.

Ryan pulled into his private parking space at the station. They left the car and hurried up the front steps. Inside, a throng of people were milling around at the front desk.

Ryan took her arm and was guiding her through the crowd, when someone called out to him.

"Ryan! They've got your boy in your office."

"Thanks, Toby."

Taking Marian's arm, he guided her down a narrow hall to a door with his name on it. A short, stocky policewoman stood up as they came in.

"Thanks, Nora."

"He's all yours, I need to get back on patrol." She nodded toward the boy hunched in a chair. "I haven't been able to get one word out of him."

Marian and Ryan looked at the boy and said in unison, "That's not Scotty."

"What? He fits your description," the officer protested. "Blond hair, small build, blue eyes and—" She pointed to a bicycle leaning against a far wall. "And riding a red bicycle."

"That could be the bicycle but he is not the missing boy."

"How can that be?" she demanded as if Ryan was somehow questioning her judgment.

"Why don't I take it from here," he suggested smoothly.

"Gladly. Here's my report." She threw down a sheet of paper and then walked out of the room.

Marian was completely at a loss. Not only was it a bitter disappointment that Scotty was still missing, but an insidious fear sluiced through her. Her thoughts tumbled in all directions. Ryan seemed sure it was the same bike. Maybe the boy would talk to her.

As if sensing she was about to take charge, he motioned to his desk chair, and his expression was an unspoken order for her to sit down. His manner made it clear this was his territory and she'd better respect it.

Pulling up another chair so that he faced the boy only a foot away, he eased down into it. Leaning back in a relaxed manner, he didn't say anything, but acted as if he had all the time in the world.

After a long three or four minutes, the scowling boy began to shift nervously. Finally he blurted out, "You know I ain't him."

"Who?"

"The kid who owns the bike."

Ryan nodded. In a rather bored voice he said, "I know that."

Another long silence.

Finally the tension was too much for the boy. "I nicked the bike."

"Oh, you stole it?" Ryan repeated in the same unhurried tone.

"Yeah."

Alarmed, Marian was ready to shake the boy to get the whole story. Had Scotty fought to keep the bike? Was he lying somewhere hurt?

"Where'd you steal it?" Ryan asked.

"At the fairgrounds."

Marian could tell from the way Ryan leaned forward that he was through wasting any more time. "Where exactly?"

"The hot-dog stand." Now that he'd begun to talk, the story poured out of him. "He leaned the bike up against the side. The way he was smiling at an old lady standing in line, I knew he was going to try to work a soft touch for some food."

"And did he?"

"Yeah, some grandma was buying him a wiener when I took off with the bike."

"All right, get yourself out of here, and the next time you're caught with sticky fingers, it'll be jail for you." Turning to Marian, he jerked his head toward the door.

"Let's go get our boy."

Chapter Seven

Rock Creek's fairgrounds were jammed. Cars, trucks, horse trailers and motorcycles were lined up for blocks. Parking would have been a challenge if Ryan hadn't shown his official badge and was directed to a private parking area behind the grandstand.

Milling crowds of people were like multicolored locusts surging in every direction. The afternoon rodeo was already in full swing, and excited shouts and yells could be heard as horse races, bronco busters and calf ropers entertained the crowd.

Ryan could tell from Marian's bewildered look that she was fearful they'd never find a small eleven-year-old boy in this maze of milling humanity.

"Let's start with the food venders. Maybe we can pick up a trail from there," Ryan said, taking her hand and holding it tightly as they pushed into the crowd.

They passed all kinds of stands selling everything from beautiful Indian rugs to gaudy hats with propellers that whirled in the wind. When they saw groups clustered around a clown, juggler or magician, they stopped and searched for a glimpse of a familiar blond head in the crowd.

"He could be anywhere," Marian said through tight lips. "Maybe he even left the grounds when he discovered his bike had been taken."

"Maybe. Maybe not," Ryan answered thoughtfully. A lot of activity was going on that could interest a boy on the loose, but how could they find him? Following good detective procedure dictated they start at the place where the missing subject was last seen.

At the hot-dog concession, Ryan asked if anyone there knew anything about a bike parked behind their stand being stolen.

"Yeah, I was here when it happened," a teenaged girl responded. "That kid was fit to be tied." She chuckled. "I learned a few cusswords. What a mouth!"

"I understand some nice lady bought him a hot dog," Ryan replied.

"Yeah, Mrs. Ferguson. She's always doing stuff like that."

"Oh, you know her."

"She goes to our church and likes kids. I heard her tell him she'd buy him a ticket to the rodeo if he calmed down."

"And did he?"

"Sure did. He seemed to forget all about the bike."

"You've been a great help. Do you know Mrs. Ferguson's full name and address?" He took out a pad and wrote down the information. He might need to check out the girl's story.

"Good job, Detective," Marian said, smiling at him gratefully.

"How would you like to take in the afternoon rodeo?" he asked, slipping an arm through hers. "I think we just might find a wide-eyed boy sitting in the grandstand."

After a half-hour search, they found Scotty sitting in the front row of the bleachers overlooking the bull-dogging area. He was yelling with the crowd, "Ride 'em, cowboy," and laughing loudly as the unfortunate rider went sailing over the animal's head.

Once Scotty was aware of Marian and Ryan standing there looking at him, the laughter instantly froze on his face. He made a quick move to get away, but Ryan's firm hand on his shoulder set him back down on the bleacher. Then, with Marian on one side and Ryan on the other, he cowered between them, tense and scowling.

Marian was torn between expressing her relief at having found him and the temptation to give him a no-nonsense lecture. When Ryan sent her a warning look, she decided not to do either.

Turning Scotty's face toward him, Ryan spoke slowly and deliberately so Scotty could read his lips. "I always like the calf roping best. Did you get to see that today?"

Scotty gave a slight nod.

"I used to practice throwing a rope," Ryan continued with an easy smile. "Never got good enough to snag anything but an old post."

Scotty kept his blue eyes fixed on Ryan's lips as if interested in what he was saying. His tense expression had eased.

"How about you, Scotty? Ever tried spinning a rope?"

Very slowly, Scotty shook his head.

"I could teach you."

"Okay."

"Good. My folks' ranch is only a couple of

miles from here. We could have our own
rodeo. How about it?"

Scotty's returning smile was answer
enough, but Marian frowned as she glanced
at her watch. Why in the world would Ryan
suggest such an outing?

"Let's go then." Ryan took Scotty's hand
as he stood up. Apparently getting to throw
a lasso himself outweighed the boy's reluctance to leave the rodeo.

Marian swallowed back a protest as they
left the bleachers. She needed to get back
and get ready for the lawyer's visit. She felt
drained and totally unsociable and irritated
with Ryan. Finally, making sure Scotty
couldn't read her lips, she lit into him.

"Why on earth are you making a pleasure
trip out of Scotty's running away?" she
demanded.

"You'd prefer that I throw the kid in
solitary confinement?"

"He shouldn't be rewarded for bad
behavior."

"You'd rather set it up so he'll run away
again?"

"No, of course not, but—"

"Marian, cool down. Scotty is an integral
part of an investigation. I have to make the

decisions on how to handle it. You'll have to trust my judgment." He leveled those steady blue eyes on her. "You do, don't you?"

She knew it was Detective Ryan Darnell who was asking the questions. Everything about his tone and facial expression advised her that any give-and-take discussion was out of the question.

"All right," she conceded rather stiffly. "May I borrow your cell phone?"

While Ryan stopped to buy a pizza and drinks for their lunch, she called Bertha's cell number.

"We found him," she told the nurse when she answered.

"Praise be! Where?"

"At a rodeo."

With a whooping laugh, Bertha said, "Doesn't that beat all? You have to love the kid's spirit."

Marian wasn't so sure about that, but was glad Bertha approved of Ryan's plan when she told her about it.

"Take your time. Everything is quiet here. Everyone's worn-out from the picnic."

She gave the nurse Ryan's cell-phone number. After she hung up, Ryan handed her a slice of pizza, and they sat down on a nearby bench to eat lunch. She couldn't help but think how ironic it was that the three of them were having a picnic lunch after all.

As Ryan drove to his parents' ranch about fifteen miles south of town, Scotty sat between them in the front seat. When Ryan pointed out some grazing horses or cattle, the boy leaned forward in the seat to see them better. Once in a while he asked a question that showed he was strictly a city boy.

Marian was familiar with his case history. Scotty had been born and raised in Denver's poorest district. Starving cats roamed the dirty, narrow alleys, and the rutted streets were filled with humanity's lowlifes. No wonder he'd been bait for street gangs and the homemade bomb that took away his hearing.

As Scotty's eager eyes followed Ryan's pointing finger, she wanted to brush back the unruly blond hair from his forehead, but she knew the lack of any expression of affection in his life would make the boy reject such an overture.

Rejection was something she'd never learned to handle well, and as she glanced at Ryan's strong profile, she realized her emotions just might be setting her up for a big one. She couldn't believe she'd be foolish enough to be physically attracted to someone who was scarcely more than a total stranger.

Ryan Darnell was a professional doing his job. She knew that. Their encounter was anything but romantic. Why would the memory of the girl in his arms continue to haunt her? Maybe it would be a good thing for her to see something of his personal life. Sometimes reality was the best antidote for romantic foolishness, she told herself.

Ryan's parents' home was set back from the main road about a half mile. Framed by tall ponderosa pine trees, the frame house had small dormer windows and a couple of brick chimneys marking the second floor, and a wide old-fashioned porch circling the front and sides. Ryan parked the car at the side of the house beside a small car.

"Looks like my sister, Ellen, is here. That's her Volvo," he told Marian. "My brother, Tom, and his wife, Angie, live here with Mom and Dad. They have two kids younger than Scotty."

As Ryan guided Scotty out of the car, he winked at him and was rewarded by a quick flash of eagerness in Scotty's eyes.

They walked to the house and Ryan barely had the front door open when a bouncy little woman in tight jeans, cotton shirt and ruffled apron was there to meet them. Her salt-and-pepper hair was pulled back in a ponytail that flopped on her neck as she motioned them inside.

"This is my mom," Ryan said with obvious affection. "Her name is Adele but everyone calls her Addie."

Her alert blue eyes were questioning as she smiled at Marian. "What a nice surprise."

Marian quickly introduced herself before Ryan could. "And this is Scotty, one of the boys in our summer program for hearing-disabled children."

"He's a whiz at reading lips," Ryan volunteered with a smile.

"Uh-oh," his mother said, chuckling. "I wouldn't want him to pick up some of the language I hear around here." Then, bending closer to Scotty so he could see her lips move, she said, "I'm glad you came to see us, Scotty. Would you like to see a brand-new baby horse?"

As Scotty nodded, Ryan asked excitedly, "Did Princess have her colt?"

"Sure did. A filly. Just after two o'clock this morning. Your dad is upstairs catching up on his sleep."

"That's my mare!" he told Marian. "I've been waiting for her to deliver."

"We thought you were on a case or we would have called you," his mother said. "Your sister told me she asked Joyce to deliver your carryall last night. I didn't know you were staying at the Wentworth estate?" she added in a questioning tone.

"Temporarily," Ryan answered briefly. Then he turned and urged Marian and Scotty back out the front door. "Come on, let's go take a look at the new arrival."

As they headed for the barn, a young collie pup joined them.

"How you doing, Laddie," Ryan greeted him affectionately, giving the pup a quick pat on the head.

"Is he your dog?" Scotty asked, frowning.

"Whenever I'm here, he is. Come on, fella."

The barn was a steep-roofed white building with a metal weather vane on the peak. Hay was piled on the high rafters, and Ryan quickly led the way to a large stall where a sorrel mare was standing patiently while a wobbly, long-legged foal nursed.

Ryan opened the stall gate and slipped inside, murmuring, "Good girl, good girl."

He patted her neck and looked her over like an anxious father.

"Have you ever seen a new baby horse before?" Marian asked Scotty as they remained outside the stall and peered over the gate.

He shook his head in a bored fashion and glanced around the barn as if looking for something more interesting. When he spied a coiled rope looped over a nearby post, his expression changed dramatically.

Immediately, Scotty darted over to the rope, lifted it off the post and fingered it. Then he brought it back to the stall to show Marian.

One thing was sure, she thought, Ryan wasn't going to get out of his promise to spend time showing Scotty how to lasso.

As she watched Ryan care for his mare, Scotty fingered the rope with a look of utter contentment. She felt strangely at odds with herself. What was she as passionate about? She couldn't think of one thing that could be considered totally personal. She realized with a kind of sad dismay that the regimented activity of her life had completely drained away this kind of spontaneous joy. The raptured look on both Ryan's and Scotty's faces made her feel like an alien.

When Ryan stepped out of the stall and saw Scotty standing there, clutching the rope with an expectant look on his face, he laughed and said, "Okay, fella. Let's find a wild fence post to lasso!"

Laddie bounded ahead of them as they headed for a nearby empty corral. While Marian leaned against the fence, watching, Ryan and Scotty worked the rope. She thought Scotty did well in his first lesson. She could tell from his face that he was pretending he was on a racing horse after a runaway colt. Ryan had been right to bring him here. Winning Scotty's confidence was worth the extra time and effort.

"That's enough for today," Ryan said after about a half hour. "But you can keep the rope, Scotty, and practice on your own."

The sun was beginning to set behind the nearby foothills as they returned and found the family gathered on a patio behind the house.

Ryan's dad, Bill Darnell, was a tall man with a rangy build and an easy smile. He wiped his hands on his apron before offering Marian a shake as Ryan introduced them. "Nice to meet you. Ryan doesn't bring his…friends around very often."

"Dad means lady friends," offered a grinning young woman.

"That's enough, sis," Ryan warned.

"He brings Joyce sometimes," a little boy about six years old said solemnly.

"They were going to get married," a girl about eight added, smiling. "I was going to be flower girl."

"That's history," Ryan said shortly. "My brother's children, Danny and Darlene. Telling all the family history. And my sister, Ellen, who is always egging them on."

"Not true," the attractive brunette said, smiling at Marian. "Ryan is responsible for all our bad habits."

"Ellen, say hello to Marian," Ryan ordered in playful mock authority.

"Hello, Marian." She searched her brother's face, obviously waiting for further information.

As Ellen's glance fell on Scotty, Marian put a hand on the boy's shoulder and quickly said, "This is Scotty, one of the boys in our summer program."

Ellen nodded. "Mom was telling us he was with you." Much to Marian's surprise, she quickly signed, "I'm happy to know you." Then she turned to Marian. "We had a deaf cousin and I knew some signing, but I'm afraid I've forgotten most of it."

Ryan's mother came out of the house at that moment and, smiling broadly, gave his father a platter of hamburger patties to grill. "You'll stay for our cookout, won't you?"

Before Marian had time to consider the invitation, Ryan's cell phone suddenly played its warning.

"I'm sorry. I have to take this." He said hello and then handed the phone to Marian. "It's for you."

She excused herself and moved to the edge of the patio, some distance away from the others, before she said, "Hello."

"It's me, Nancy. Bertha didn't want to call, but I thought we should. I'm sorry to—"

"It's all right," Marian quickly assured her. Nancy's tone told her something was wrong. "What is it?"

"Arthur Kennedy is in town. He just called from the hotel and said he's coming out this evening after dinner to check on things. I didn't tell him where you were or that you'd been chasing a runaway all afternoon. I lied and said you were gone taking care of some kind of business— which I guess was the truth in a way. I wasn't sure you wanted him to know we'd lost a kid."

"You did the right thing," Marian quickly assured her as she silently swore. Her dealings with the Denver lawyer had never been the greatest. Arthur Kennedy had made it clear on several occasions that a more experienced administrator would have been his choice for director of the program. How easily he could turn this whole situation into cause for her dismissal. She knew she should have gone right back to prepare for his visit.

"We'll leave right away. Thanks for the red alert."

Ryan must have been watching her take the call, because he went over to her the minute she hung up. As she gave the phone back to him, her expression must have been readable because he worriedly demanded, "What's up?"

When she told him about the Denver lawyer's visit, he muttered something under his breath. "I was hoping we'd have at least another day or two to verify or disprove Scotty's story. I don't see any other choice but to level with him."

No doubt the lawyer would think she'd handled the whole situation in the worst possible way, and at the moment, she was inclined to agree with him.

Ryan made their excuses for having to leave. "Business," he said shortly. Apparently they were used to his abrupt comings and goings because they didn't question him.

Scotty had been sitting on the grass, playing with the dog. When they told him it was time to leave, he just continued to stroke Laddie's soft fur.

"I'm not going," he said with childish determination. "I'm going to stay with Laddie."

Marian was ready to reach down and help the boy to his feet, but Ryan stopped her. Bending down, he looked Scotty right in the eyes.

"Laddie likes you, Scotty. And you like Laddie, right?"

Scotty nodded, his eyes narrowing suspiciously.

"Since he's my dog, maybe he could go with you for a visit. You'd have to feed him and make sure he stayed out of trouble. Do you think you could do that?"

Scotty nodded vigorously. "I can watch him."

"Good, let's go."

Marian stared at both of them in stunned

silence. When Ryan straightened up, she faced him directly, her back to Scotty and the dog, and demanded, "What in the world are you thinking? A dog? I can't look after—"

"You don't have to. I'll see to it Laddie doesn't cause anyone any trouble." Then he added simply, "The boy needs someone to love."

She didn't realize it at the time, but it was at that moment that she fell in love with Detective Ryan Darnell.

Chapter Eight

They put Scotty in the backseat with the dog as they drove to the estate. Marian had little to say to Ryan as her thoughts whirled like an off-balance gyroscope. She'd spent the afternoon anxiously searching for a runaway, and now the arrival of the Denver lawyer put her emotions in another vise. She had no idea how to handle the present situation.

As if Ryan were reading her thoughts, he gave her a reassuring smile. "Hey, don't look as if you're headed for the guillotine. It's going to be all right. Why don't you fill me in on this Arthur Kennedy. What's his background?"

"His father was the lawyer for Alva Wentworth's millionaire husband. Arthur took his place after his father's death and remained as Alva's legal advisor when she became a widow."

"How old is he?"

"Oh, I'd say around fifty. Very proper and all business. He's in political circles and in line for appointment as a federal judge. He always guards his time like a miser hoarding gold. I've never felt comfortable in his presence," she admitted.

"I need more time to verify Scotty's story one way or another," he admitted. "I talked with Toby Bower this morning and he said they're beginning to run the fingerprints through the Automated Fingerprint Identification System. He'll let us know if we get a hit. But even if we do, the prints will probably belong to people who have had a legit reason for being in the cabin."

"And?"

"We're back to square one." His jaw tightened as he muttered, "There has to be something more. Something we're missing."

"And what about Scotty?" she asked him. "If you verify he's lied about this whole thing, I'll never be able to keep him in the program. Kennedy was negative about accepting a kid off the street in the first place, and the foundation board will listen to his recommendation, especially now that the boy has been a runaway." She sighed. "Scotty will go back to the city and become one more lost kid."

"We have to make sure that doesn't happen."

How simple he made it sound. At the moment she was trying to figure out how to explain to her staff why a runaway boy deserved the gift of a dog. Obviously, Ryan was used to taking matters into his own hands. He must not realize that she didn't have that luxury.

Going back in her mind over everything that had happened, she still felt calling the authorities had seemed the right thing to do. Now, she was having second thoughts about agreeing to his lies about being on the premises. And what was worse, she was allowing her own feelings to be manipulated by the situation.

When they reached the mansion and got out of the car, Marian said firmly, "We'll have to have some rules about the dog. I believe Mrs. Wentworth had a dog at one time, but I'll need to check that the rest of the staff isn't allergic. In the meantime, there's a kennel off the kitchen in the servants' quarters. Laddie can sleep there and use the small doggie door to the outside." She paused, suddenly assailed by the complications a pet was bound to entail. "Since you have Scotty's confidence, you should be the one to make sure he understands."

Ryan nodded. "I'll see to it."

"I have some business matters to attend to before Kennedy gets here. You and Scotty are on your own."

She turned away and walked swiftly into the mansion and straight down the hall to her office. She could hear the children leaving the dining room and heading for their evening quota of Disneyland.

She sat down at her desk and tried to figure out exactly what position to take when the lawyer got there. First of all, she needed to get his authorization for including some new expenditures in the budget. She wanted to hire a full-time aide to prepare materials that the teachers and nurse needed. Elsie still wanted a paid helper in the kitchen. And then there was the field trip to Mesa Verde National Park to view the Indian ruins. She'd itemized expenses that she needed approved. Ziller had offered to drive the bus—for a generous fee, of course.

And she should probably mention Laddie. As much as she hated to do it, Kennedy expected to know everything that happened at the Wentworth estate.

When she had finished organizing her report, she leaned back in her chair and took a deep breath and let her thoughts shift to the immediate problem of how much to tell Kennedy about Ryan Darnell.

She knew Ryan was foremost a dedicated police officer, and doing his job wouldn't be influenced by the personal ramifications of anyone who stood in the way of an investigation. Not her. Not her job. Not her future. The fallout from his investigation wasn't his paramount concern at the moment. If the boy had stumbled onto a murder scene, he needed to prepare some groundwork for possible suspects. She knew all of that. Still, she wished to heaven she wasn't about to face Kennedy with a bunch of lies.

"Oh, so you're back," Nancy said as she came in the office. "Lady, you look awful," she commented with her usual honesty.

"I feel awful."

"I thought everything was under control. Scotty is back safe and sound and things ran smoothly today while you were chasing the runaway." After Marion mentioned the dog, Nancy nodded her approval and said she'd check with the rest of the staff. "Don't you think you should spruce up a bit before the Big Gun gets here?"

An appropriate nickname for the lawyer, Marian thought. As she got to her feet, she felt like someone about to be lined up against a wall and interrogated.

"Wear that soft violet summer dress with the low neck," Nancy suggested with a wink. "The old boy will forget all about rules and regulations."

"I doubt that." Kennedy had always been polite, listening carefully to what she had to say, and then giving his decision in an unhurried but firm way that brooked no argument.

"You'd better shake a leg," Nancy said, looking at her watch. "Kennedy said he'd be here at seven. You've got forty-five minutes to get beautiful."

"It may take a tad longer than that," Marian replied dryly. Playing the vamp had never been her style. Even though she knew some men found her attractive, she'd never counted on looks to get her past anything in life.

She went straight to her room and thankfully closed the door behind her. She wondered if Ryan and Scotty had gone to the kitchen to get something to eat. Her stomach was growling, reminding her that the pizza she'd had for lunch wasn't going to sustain her for the ordeal ahead. She'd have to make do with some fruit and cheese and crackers she had around for snacking.

As she quickly bathed and changed clothes, she decided she wasn't going to follow Nancy's suggestion and dress up at all. In fact, she decided that looking more like a plain, dedicated career woman might be the way to go.

She wasn't sure that she'd obtained the right effect as she looked in the mirror. The two-piece linen suit was a soft beige with brown piping on the collar and short sleeves, but the only blouse she'd ever worn with it was a soft pink. Pulling her hair into a clip at the back of her head instead of letting it flow free the way she usually did, she thought the professional middle-aged man might approve of her appearance.

The children were still in the living room watching a movie when she hurriedly made her way back to the office at fifteen minutes before seven. She'd quickly learned that Kennedy was always annoyingly punctual for any meeting. Her hope to have a few minutes to collect her wits before he arrived was dashed when she heard men's voices coming from the office.

As she paused in the doorway, she saw that Kennedy was already there. He was sitting at her desk, and had his briefcase open in front of him. What took her breath away was Ryan sitting relaxed in a chair beside the desk.

"There you are," he greeted her, quickly rising to his feet. His smile had a hint of a warning in it. "Mr. Kennedy and I have been getting acquainted."

"Good evening, Marian." The lawyer also rose to his feet. As always, he was impeccably dressed in a dark suit, tie, white shirt with cuff links and polished shoes. His graying hair was carefully cut to help hide a thinning spot.

"Am I late?" she asked innocently, knowing damn well she wasn't.

"Not at all," he assured her. "I arrived a little early and Mr. Darnell has been bringing me up to date on the house-security check. Sounds like a necessary expenditure, Marian, but I was surprised that you had not waited for budget approval before engaging him."

"I guess that will come when I make my recommendations for new hardware and procedures," Ryan intervened smoothly.

Marian knew then he was sticking to his fabricated identity. Somehow he had presented it so Kennedy had accepted it.

Relief was short-lived.

"What about that boy, Scotty Tanner?" Kennedy demanded, frowning. "I've always had my doubts about him. You can't take delinquents off the street and expect acceptable behavior. I'm glad you were here, Ryan, when he decided to take a bicycle ride this afternoon."

So Ryan had told him about Scotty taking off on his bike.

Marian sat down weakly in the only other empty chair. Kennedy had not offered to relinquish the one behind her desk.

"No problem. He didn't get far," Ryan replied, making it sound as if it had been a short little joy ride.

Marian was astonished at the bald-faced lie, but the lawyer seemed ready to move on to other important matters.

"Shall we go over the projected budget and program, Marian? I have to meet with Mrs. Wentworth and get her approval for any changes, you know."

Ryan immediately excused himself. "I'll leave you two to the business at hand. I want to check out a couple of doors on the servants' side of the house. We shouldn't leave any entry without some kind of security alarm."

Kennedy nodded in agreement. "We don't want anyone coming or going from the house without detection. You have my authority to look into it and I'll expect your full report as soon as possible."

Marian was astonished how deftly Ryan had handled the situation in a way that had saved her—at least for the present.

As she and Kennedy went over the report she'd prepared for him, she began to feel confident again and was able to stand firm on her recommendations.

"You'd have to take up hiring another staff member with Mrs. Wentworth. I promised her we would not exceed the proposed budget," he said as he closed his briefcase. "As for the field-trip expenses, they're included in extracurricular activities. And the dog can stay, unless he becomes a problem."

"All right, I'll arrange a visit to Mrs. Wentworth. I've been wanting to express my appreciation for the use of her estate."

She walked with Kennedy to the front door and breathed a sigh of relief as he drove away. She could hear muffled sounds from the floors above, telling her the children were settling in for the night.

She went back to the office and had just cleared her desk when Ryan appeared in the doorway.

"Good, he's gone."

"Just left."

"I've got something to show you. I think you'll be pleased." His smile was suddenly a trifle uncertain. "At least I hope you are."

She hated the way her stomach automatically tightened. She didn't like surprises. Being in control of one's life meant surprises weren't allowed. "What is it?"

"You'll see. Come on." He pulled her to her feet and slipped an arm through hers.

As he led her down the hall to the kitchen, she was certain he'd fixed something to eat or drink and she didn't feel like either. She was bone tired. She wondered why he wasn't upstairs with Scotty. And what had he done with the dog?

When they reached the kitchen, she had her answer to both. Scotty was drinking a glass of milk, already dressed in his pajamas, and Laddie was eating something from Elsie's hand as she fed him. Scotty grinned at her with a milk mustache and Elsie laughed as Laddie licked her hand to get the last juicy morsel.

Ryan was looking at her as if he was expecting her approval. Maybe she'd been in Kennedy's company too recently to immediately throw out all the rules and regulations that she'd helped put in place to keep the summer program running smoothly and efficiently. All the children were to be in bed in their assigned rooms by curfew. They ate at mealtime, not in between. How could she get control of Scotty if he was allowed to break all the rules?

"Since Scotty, Laddie and I seemed destined to be temporary roommates, it would be wise for us to stay in one of the unoccupied servant rooms until…" He silently finished the sentence with a knowing nod.

"I'd be damn glad of the company," Elsie spoke up. "I hate this big old house with all its squeaks and moans. Having a dog around would put my mind at ease. That's for sure."

They waited for her answer. What could she say? Nothing. Nothing at all. Marian managed a feeble smile of surrender. "All right, I'll tell Rob about the change."

"Good," Ryan said. "Now you'd better get some rest yourself."

"I think I will. Good night." She had taken a few steps toward the door, when a small hand suddenly touched hers.

"Night," said Scotty.

As she looked into his deep eyes, she could see they were happy and shining in a way she'd never seen before. Suddenly she knew that keeping him safe was worth breaking all the rules and regulations in the whole wide world.

Chapter Nine

As soon as Scotty was safely seated in Rob's class the next morning, Ryan went back to their room and let Laddie out for a run. He was satisfied that he had taken the right precaution in bunking with Scotty and the dog until they could verify or discard the boy's story. A gut feeling told him the boy wasn't lying, but he needed more than that to justify spending his time at the mansion. Not that being around an attractive, sexually appealing woman like Marian was a hardship, he admitted to himself. The more he was around her, the more he wanted to get to know her better. There was a depth to her that intrigued him. She was dedicated, intelligent and totally feminine. A dangerous combination. He might be in danger of giving his heart to someone who didn't want it.

Sitting down on a back step while Laddie

sniffed his way around the immediate surroundings, Ryan called Toby on his cell phone. He knew he was pushing the limited facilities of the local forensic lab with his demands, but he had confidence that Toby would find something—if there was something to be found.

"What's the good word, buddy?" Ryan asked.

"Oh, you're a mind reader, are you?" Toby teased.

"You have something for me?"

"Don't know. Maybe. We hit on one set of fingerprints. Let's see here," he said as the sound of rustling papers told Ryan he was looking for the information.

Ryan's jaw tightened as he waited impatiently.

"Oh, yes, here it is. Victor Blaise. He was arrested in an investigation of a petty larceny robbery last year. Got off with six months' incarceration."

The caretaker's nephew!

"Mean anything?" Toby asked at Ryan's pointed silence.

"Maybe, maybe not," Ryan replied slowly. "But it's verification that he was in the cabin."

"Not in the cabin," Toby corrected. "The matching prints were on the front windowsill."

"What?"

"Nothing on the doorknobs, either. Strange, isn't it? Even the boy's small prints weren't there. Someone must have wiped them clean after Scotty ran away."

"If it was Victor, he could have forgotten about the windowsill," Ryan speculated. "Or he could have been snooping around the cabin even a day or two earlier, and when he found the doors locked, he went on his way."

"Some of the prints we have are too smeared to give us any kind of clear reading. Someone could have wiped off the doorknobs later and not known about Victor's prints on the windowsill."

"If we knew who that someone was, I bet we could link him to a missing body. At the moment we still don't have anything except Scotty's story to validate the cabin as a crime scene."

"You're still holding to the belief that the boy is telling the truth?"

"I'd bet my badge on it. Thanks, Toby. Keep me posted."

"You're still at the estate?"

"For the time being."

"That must be rough. Keeping company with a beautiful woman in deluxe accommodations like that."

"You better believe it," Ryan quipped. "All in the line of duty."

"Some duty," Toby said in a teasing tone as he hung up.

For several minutes Ryan sat on the step with his arms resting on his knees while he digested the new information. Victor Blaise had a felony record. Then he stood up and headed for the garage with the dog bounding along at his heels.

Elsie had adopted Laddie and it was obvious the cook was an animal lover. The dog's tail never quit wagging when she talked to him and spoiled him with food and attention.

As Ryan climbed the steps to the garage apartment, he was hoping he'd have a chance to talk to Victor alone without his uncle being there. The caretaker had made it clear he didn't want Ryan on the premises for any reason.

As luck would have it, Henry answered Ryan's knock. A deep furrowed frown was his only greeting.

"Is Victor around?" Ryan asked as he glanced through the open doorway.

"Whatcha want him for?"

"I have some questions."

"About what?"

"Is he here?" Ryan sidestepped the question.

"Nope."

Ryan wanted to pull out his badge and thrust it in the man's face, but he forced himself to smile. "Do you know where I can find him?"

Henry's jaw hardened. "Damned if I know where he went. He took off on his motorcycle yesterday noon when everyone was at the picnic."

"When do you expect him back?"

"I don't. His carryall is gone," Henry said, moving away from the open door.

Ryan entered with Laddie at his heels. "And he didn't give you any idea where he was going?"

"Hell, no."

When Laddie started sniffing at an open closet door, Henry moved quickly to close it. Before he could, Ryan glimpsed several shelves filled with objects that could have come from the big house. Maybe Ziller had been helping himself while the place had been vacant. At the moment, petty theft wasn't at the top of Ryan's list of concerns.

"Has Victor been bumming off of you all

summer?" he asked the caretaker in a sympathetic tone.

"Naw, just a couple of weeks."

"That's a long time to have a freeloader underfoot. I guess if the house hadn't been occupied, he could have stayed there or at the cabin."

"No way! I couldn't trust him not to lift everything in sight in the big house and the cabin's been closed up ever since Mrs. Wentworth had her cleaning service give it a going over just before you guys moved in. I wasn't about to let Victor have free rein in either place. I know him too well." He glanced around the untidy apartment. "He never lifted a finger to help around here."

Ryan nodded sympathetically.

Ziller scowled. "What was it you wanted with him?"

"Oh, I thought he might want to earn a few bucks helping me out," Ryan lied. "You know, climbing up into the dusty attic checking on some wiring or crawling around the dirty basement." He tried to make the job as unattractive as possible so Henry wouldn't volunteer.

He didn't.

"I guess the old lady is getting nervous

with all the kids being here," Ryan said thoughtfully.

"All this hype about checking out security is a bunch of hogwash," Henry snapped. "All the years I've been on the job, there hasn't been a burglary. Hell, I've got a rifle ready and loaded if anybody tries anything." A warning flashed in his gray eyes.

It was clear to Ryan that the man was ready and willing to spill as much blood as necessary to protect his own interests at the Wentworth estate. If Scotty was right, he might have already killed someone to prove it.

Ryan left without gaining any more information about where Victor had gone. Maybe he was still in town. Maybe miles away by now. There was a logical explanation for Victor's fingerprints on the windowsill—he was snooping to see what was inside. Without any evidence that a crime had been committed, Ryan couldn't put out an APB to bring him back.

There has to be something more, Ryan told himself as he and the dog headed through the trees in the direction of the cabin. For nearly an hour he made wider and wider circles around the area, searching for anything that might show that someone had dragged a body away and buried it in the nearby rocks and thick drifts of trees. Laddie explored the ravines and hillside. Ryan was pretty sure if there was anything dead within sniffing distance, the dog would find it.

After nearly an hour, nothing.

Frustrated and disappointed, he returned to the mansion and was just going inside, when he got another call on his cell phone.

"Yes, Chief," he responded readily when his superior, Chief Peterson, identified himself. Even though Ryan had submitted the proper reports explaining his reasons for providing protection at the Wentworth estate, he was surprised he hadn't heard from the chief sooner.

"I just checked with Toby and he tells me he has a print match on a fellow who's been hanging around the Wentworth estate. A Victor Blaise?"

"That's right."

"Well, we just got a call from a pawnshop proprietor who suspects a guy identified as Victor Blaise is trying to hawk some expensive gold-plated animal figurines. He claims they were gifts from his uncle who handles the Wentworth estate."

"I don't think 'handles' is the correct word. His uncle is caretaker there. And I think Blaise probably stole the stuff yesterday." Ryan's thoughts raced ahead. "Will you pull him in? This will give me a chance to interrogate him."

"Okay, but you better get something solid soon, Ryan, or I'm going to have to assign you to something else."

"Yes, sir. I understand."

Ryan left Laddie with Elsie. Then he went directly to Marian's office and was glad he didn't have to search the premises for her. She was sitting at her desk, with several piles of papers in front of her and a pair of reading glasses perched on her nose.

"Everything's under control," he assured her quickly when she peered at him over the rims of her glasses. "I just have to go to the office, and I wanted to make sure that Scotty has someone riding herd on him while I'm gone."

She pulled off her glasses and searched his face as he bent over the desk. "Is there something happening that I should know about?"

"I'll fill you in when I get back," he promised. "You'll see to Scotty?"

Nodding, she replied, "I'll be his study-hall monitor."

"Good." Impulsively he reached out and squeezed her hand. "As my mother always says, keep the faith."

She smiled at him, and he turned and left before he gave in to a mounting impulse to draw her to her feet and kiss her.

By the time Ryan got to the station, Victor was sitting in a small interrogation room. His scowl deepened when Ryan walked in. "What the hell are you doing here?"

Ryan slid easily into a chair opposite him. "The question is what are you doing, Victor? Trying to hock stolen goods?"

"I didn't steal nothing!"

"Where did you get the stuff that made the pawnbroker suspicious enough to call the police?"

Victor shifted nervously. "My uncle gave it to me."

"Really?"

"Yeah, he's got a bunch of stuff like that," he spat.

"A closetful?"

Victor suddenly went pale. "He'll kill me if I put the law on him."

Ryan quickly shifted gears. He wasn't

interested in convicting Victor or his uncle of petty theft. "We have your fingerprints on the front window of the cabin, Victor." Ryan leaned forward. "You'd better tell me what in the hell happened there."

Victor gave him such a blank look that Ryan was pretty sure he wasn't faking it. "What do you mean?"

"You were at the cabin. You went inside and—"

"I did not. The place was locked up."

"When was this?"

"A few days ago. I looked in a couple of windows and that was that!"

"You didn't see anyone around? Or anything worth stealing?"

"Naw," he answered before he realized Ryan had tricked him. "I tell you I ain't stole nothing. Just ask my uncle."

"I think we will." Ryan walked out of the room and told the guard at the door, "Keep him locked up until I check out his story."

When he told Toby why he had Victor Blaise locked up, the forensic detective asked, "Do you think the uncle gave him the stuff?"

"No, and that's why I want you to call Ziller and tell him why the police have his nephew in custody. I can't do it because I don't want Ziller to know I'm connected with the police."

Toby nodded. "If we can charge Victor with theft, we may be able to keep him around long enough to get some information he may not even know he has."

Ryan waited while Toby went into his office and made the call. It was an unwritten courtesy not to eavesdrop on another officer's interrogation. Through the glass window, Ryan could see him talking and knew he'd reached the caretaker.

When Toby came out of his office, he was shaking his head. "I know Victor Blaise's uncle is lying, but he swears he gave the things to his nephew. Something about a promise he'd made to his sister to look after him. When I asked Ziller where he got the expensive items in the first place, he claimed that for every year of service, Mrs. Wentworth gave him an animal figure for his collection. What's more he has gift cards from her to prove it." Toby sighed. "I'm afraid you've no legal cause to detain Victor."

"Once we release him, he'll be long gone and so will any information he might have given us."

Toby sighed again. "What else is new?"

MARIAN'S MORNING had been one of those frustrating start-and-stop affairs. She had decided her top priority was following through on getting Mrs. Wentworth's approval to increase the staff with a teacher's aide. She was gathering information from the school district about finding a qualified person for the job, when she was interrupted at noon by the two weekly cleaning ladies stopping by her office.

Since her residence in the nursing home, Mrs. Wentworth had engaged a cleaning service to make sure the house was kept up to the standard she had always expected.

Obviously frustrated trying to carry out their usual schedule with the place full of kids and the rooms being used for a variety of different activities, Marian doubted if the same two maids would show up regularly as the summer went on.

She braced herself for a parcel of complaints, and the older, husky woman, Gertie, had plenty of them. The younger woman, Edna, only nodded and pursed her mouth in agreement.

Gertie unloaded their displeasure about the conditions of the bathrooms and crowded bedrooms, and all the interruptions that made it impossible to do everything that Mrs. Wentworth had on her list.

Marian wasn't about to get between the cleaning ladies and Mrs. Wentworth's orders. "Just follow your usual routine as best you can," she advised.

"And as if the mansion isn't enough," Gertie went on, "Mrs. Wentworth wants us to make sure the cabin is kept ready for use." Drawing herself up in an indignant stance, she said, "I suppose it's just as messy?"

Marian stiffened as she quickly answered, "No, it's fine. You don't have to spend any time on it until I let you know."

Gertie nodded. "Good, we'll cross that off the list."

She knew Ryan would be furious if she let these women do anything to the cabin, inside or out. And if anyone discovered the police were interested in the place, there would be a lot of questions floating around.

"You cleaned it before we got here, didn't you?" Marian couldn't resist asking. "I mean, you swept, dusted, and polished the furniture?"

Marian didn't know where she was going with this and wished to heaven Ryan was asking the questions.

"We know our job," Gertie responded, looking a little insulted.

"I was wondering about…about the floors."

"Always a mess. Aren't they, Edna? We mopped and waxed the whole place. Cleaned that Navajo rug and—"

"Navajo rug?" Marian echoed. "Where'd you put it?"

"We never move anything," Edna spoke up in a defensive voice. "We laid it right back down where it belonged."

"And where was that?" Somehow Marian knew even before the woman answered what she was going to say.

"Why, in front of the fireplace, of course. That's where it's always been."

Chapter Ten

Marian was standing in the front hall with the cleaning ladies who were just leaving when Ryan returned to the house. When she saw him, she quickly excused herself from the two women and motioned for him to follow her into the sunroom.

He wondered what had put the spark of excitement in her eyes. After she shut the door behind them, she took a deep breath and said excitedly, "There was a rug. There was a rug." She said it twice as if he wasn't getting the message.

"A rug?"

"At the cabin. In front of the fireplace," she explained impatiently. "Didn't you say there was nothing there but bare floor when you checked out Scotty's story?"

"Yes, that's right," he answered with a

quick nod. "Toby didn't find any sign that one had ever been there."

"Well, according to the maids, they put a Navajo rug in front of the fireplace as usual the last time they cleaned."

"Good work!" He knew the rug could have prevented any evidence from reaching the floor. "Now we have something tangible pointing to a crime scene—if we can establish that no one else innocently removed the rug."

"Why would they?"

Ryan thought about Victor's sticky fingers and the things he'd stolen from his uncle, but a Navajo rug didn't seem to promise any quick money. Whoever removed a body in a rug would need better transportation than a motorcycle.

Aloud, he said, "Sometime between when Scotty ran away and you arrived to check out his story, the body and rug could have been removed from the cabin."

As Marian shivered, he gently lifted her chin and eased back a soft reddish-blond tendril framing her face. He knew the pressure was only likely to get worse with every bit of evidence that supported Scotty's testimony. He wished there was some way to spare her.

Taking a deep breath, she pulled away from his embrace. "I told the cleaning ladies to leave the cabin alone. What do we do now?"

"I guess you do your job and I do mine," he said as evenly as he could. The thought of putting her through the kind of misery that murder brought with it made him wish he'd never been a detective. If there had been a homicide, she was going to be right in the middle of it and there was nothing he could do to change that.

She moved away from him toward her desk as if needing a moment to compose herself. "I have to make a trip to the nursing home in the morning and talk to Mrs. Wentworth about adding an aide to the staff. I was wrong about my having the time to help the two teachers with the hands-on activities. There are more demands on my time than I expected."

"Why don't I drive you. I'll need to talk to Toby about this new information and check in with my chief."

"What about Scotty?"

"We could leave him at my parents' ranch for a couple of hours while we tend to business. My dad could keep a close eye on him. Maybe even give him his second roping lesson."

A weak smile eased the tension in her face. "All right. I can be ready to leave by ten o'clock."

THE NEXT MORNING, Marian dressed carefully for her first meeting with the wealthy benefactor whose home she was occupying. From the moment she had arrived, she'd been aware of an aura of wealth, good taste and bountiful living that permeated every inch of the mansion and grounds.

Her own upbringing had been strictly middle-class. She had parents who had been hardworking teachers with limited salaries. Because they had accepted teaching contracts in several different states and overseas, she'd never known a permanent home. She couldn't help but envy Ryan's deep roots in one place. As far as she knew, the only time he'd lived away from Rock Creek was when he was in law-enforcement training in Denver.

As she chose her outfit for the day, she wondered if Alva Wentworth would expect the director of the summer program to wear something reserved and tailored. A brown shirtwaist dress and serviceable oxfords might be a good choice. On the other hand, if she was going to be spending part of the day with the handsome Ryan Darnell, she decided something more flattering might be in order.

One glance in the mirror after she had made her selection warned Marian that she might have chosen the wrong outfit to impress the wealthy widow. A soft royal-blue skirt swirled nicely over her hips and harmonized with a soft floral blouse in summer colors. Her high-heel white shoes were scarcely more than crossed straps holding her feet in place, but they'd give her the height and confidence she needed to face the widow.

She'd applied only a light lip gloss and a hint of eye shadow, but there was a heightened color in her face. And she knew why. It wasn't the widow Wentworth she was out to impress.

When she met Ryan and Scotty at the car, the detective smiled his approval. As he opened the door for her, he bent close to her earlobe and murmured, "Nice perfume."

Scotty sat in the backseat with the dog, and his usual belligerent frown was absent as he followed Ryan's instructions to buckle up.

"What about Laddie?" the boy demanded. "He ain't got a belt."

"They haven't made dog belts yet," Ryan replied. "I guess you'll have to keep hold of him in case I have to stop suddenly."

"Okay," Scotty replied as he coaxed Laddie to lie across his lap so he could pet him.

Ryan and Marian exchanged quick smiles. She was glad that Rob had reported that Scotty was behaving considerably better than usual. The teacher said he'd even volunteered some sign language to communicate with a couple of the other boys. Rob wasn't quite sure what he was trying to tell the boys, but it had something to do with roping. Scotty's enthusiastic demonstration had made that quite clear.

As Ryan drove to the Sunny Acres Complex in Rock Creek, Marian saw that it was built on a mesa slightly higher than the rest of the town. The stone buildings included traditional nursing-home facilities but also several retirement lodges and individual cottages for senior citizens who needed a protective environment.

As Ryan let her out at the entrance of the main building, he asked, "How long do you think you'll be?"

"It depends. If Mrs. Wentworth is taking a morning nap, it might be a couple of hours."

"No problem." He handed her a card. "Just call this number when you're through. I'll be at the precinct. Good luck." As he gave her a reassuring smile, he squeezed her hand. "I hope you get what you want."

She quickly went inside, and her high heels echoed on the marble floor as she approached the reception counter.

"I'm here to see Mrs. Wentworth," Marian told a stern-looking, middle-aged woman wearing black horn-rimmed glasses.

"Do you have an appointment?"

Marian wasn't sure she'd heard correctly. "An appointment?"

"You have to clear a visit with Alva Wentworth through her personal secretary," the receptionist explained rather abruptly. "Does Miss Tilman know about your coming?"

"No," Marian replied in an even, unhurried tone. "Mrs. Wentworth's Denver lawyer, Mr. Kennedy, recommended the visit. I'm the director of the children's program at the Wentworth estate this summer."

Marian was rewarded with a slight lift of the woman's eyebrows as she digested this information. "All right. I'll give Miss Tilman a call at the cottage."

"Thank you."

Marian was amazed that the wealthy lived in a world of protocol that even reached into a nursing home. Suddenly, she wished that she'd waited until Arthur Kennedy could have come with her. A feeling of being an intruder at the wealthy woman's home and estate came over her. In some strange way, she felt she might be taken to task for it.

As the receptionist spoke into the telephone, Marian couldn't tell from her expression what the exchange might be about. When the woman hung up the phone, she walked back to the desk and handed Marian a pen and an open ledger.

"Sign in, please. Miss Tilman will meet you in a few minutes. You may wait in the reception area." She nodded toward the archway at the end of a short hall.

When Marian came into the large room, several people were there. Some in wheelchairs and others just sitting near the windows, looking out. All the conversation was hushed and Marian was thankful for the deep tufted carpet that muffled the click of her high heels.

Sinking into an overstuffed wing chair close to the door, she was grateful for a few minutes to collect herself. Several times she had visited other nursing-home facilities but none of them had had this exclusive-country-club ambience.

One thing was certain, Marian decided while she was waiting, she wasn't going to kowtow to any better-than-you-are snobbishness. Mr. Kennedy had given her the impression that he wasn't about to ask the wealthy Mrs. Wentworth to increase the approved budget. In fact, the lawyer's behavior had hinted that he might be afraid of the old woman.

When a smartly dressed woman in a white linen suit came through the door, Marian was pretty sure she must be Alva's personal secretary. Her brown hair was cut short, and gold earrings matched a simple brooch on her lapel. She carried her height and solid build well.

"Ruth Tilman," she said as she walked over to where Marian was sitting. "I've been intending to come out to the estate and meet you, Miss Richards."

"And I've been wanting to visit Mrs. Wentworth and thank her for her generosity," Marian replied smoothly in the same tone as she rose to her feet. "She's been very gracious and supportive of our program. I hope this isn't too much of an intrusion."

"Her cottage is just across the square. Shall

we?" She gave an inviting sweep of her hand, and a ruby ring flashing on her right index finger verified her position paid well.

"Yes, thank you, Miss Tilman," Marian responded. "I promise not to take up much of her time."

As they followed a path through the well-landscaped grounds, Marian wasn't surprised when Alva Wentworth's cottage, complete with private garden, turned out to be twice as large as any other in the complex.

A private nurse in uniform met them at the door.

"Is she…?" Miss Tilman asked the young woman as they went inside.

"Waiting in the sitting room," the nurse replied. "She insisted on having tea set out with cake even though it's just midmorning." Her worried expression implied that this kind of entertainment was not on the elderly woman's medical agenda. "I've reminded her that she needs her morning rest. She's been awake and fussy since dawn."

"I'll only stay a few minutes," Marian promised.

The young nurse's manner indicated she was less than confident about being in charge of the situation. Marian suspected she'd been the loser in an earlier head-to-head confrontation with the wealthy Alva Wentworth.

The nurse led the way to a fashionably furnished room where the elderly woman was sitting in a high-back wicker chair as if holding court in front of a regal audience. Her silk lavender Oriental robe fell softly above petite silver slippers, and her white hair was pulled high on her head, showing tiny diamond studs in her ears.

Marian had the absurd feeling she should bow or at least kiss the withered hand held out to her as the wealthy woman greeted her. "How nice of you to come, Miss Richards."

Marian replied quickly, "I'm honored to meet you, Mrs. Wentworth. Your generosity has meant so much to our children."

"I'm glad the estate is being put to good use," Alva responded in a strong voice that was at odds with her slight frame. "Please have a seat. Ruth, will you please pour and pass the tea cakes?"

Marian certainly didn't feel like a tea party, but she played the part expected of her. She responded politely in a positive tone to all the questions put to her.

Ruth Tilman was especially intent upon quizzing her about the responsibilities of directing such a program. Marian felt she gave a good account of herself, but the way Mrs. Wentworth's sharp eyes narrowed as she listened made Marian think that she knew everything was not running as smoothly as Marian pretended.

Setting down her cup on the side table, Alva asked Marian directly, "What was it you wanted to see me about?"

Marian knew that the old lady had not been fooled into thinking this was a social visit. Probably most people who took the time to visit her wanted something. Marian was ashamed that she was one of those. She regretted not having come earlier to introduce herself and make friends with her benefactor.

"After a week into our program, I realized that we are short of staff even for only twelve students. An addition of an aide would help enormously since there is a great deal of material that has to be prepared daily. I spoke to Mr. Kennedy about it last evening and he seemed to agree. If you approve adding this expenditure, I'm sure we could get an experienced teacher's aide through the local school system."

Before Alva had a chance to reply, Ruth spoke up in a confrontational tone. "Miss

Richards, the budget that was approved was considered quite generous for the number of students determined by that enrollment. Most classroom sizes are twenty-five to thirty, not twelve pupils, handicapped or not."

Marian was startled by the censure in her manner. One would have thought that every additional dollar came out of her pocket.

"That's true, Miss Tilman, but most classrooms are in session six hours a day, not twenty-four," Marian replied as evenly as she could.

Alva chuckled. "Ruth, dear. I suspect twelve students around the clock would challenge even your magnificent ability to cope."

"I'm not a teacher," she replied stiffly and pointedly.

"Exactly, and that's why we should follow the advice of those who are. It seems that an aide might be very appropriate under the circumstances." She ignored her secretary's disapproving intake of breath. "Hire your aide, Miss Richards, and I will advise Mr. Kennedy of the increased budget." Then she leaned slightly forward and asked eagerly, "Are the children enjoying the ponies?"

Marian thought she hadn't heard correctly. "Ponies?"

Her secretary quickly intervened. "There aren't any horses left at the estate. Remember?"

Alva frowned. "Oh, yes. That's a shame." Then she added regretfully, "Stanley, my grandson, always loved riding the ponies." Her eyes wandered to a nearby table where a young man's photograph was placed. "I wish things had gone differently with my grandson," she said, sighing. "I always thought it would be Stanley's children who would be enjoying the estate."

Marian tried to remember what Ryan had said about the conflict between the grandson and his grandmother. Something about her disowning him because he'd tried to get his hands on his inheritance before she died.

"He would have filled up the mansion, all right," Ruth said with obvious scorn. "With all his low-life buddies."

"Maybe he would have changed…in time. I shouldn't have disowned him."

Touched by the loneliness in the woman's voice and the sudden slump in her thin shoulders, Marian asked impulsively, "Could you make a visit to the estate, Mrs. Wentworth, and see the difference your kindness is making in the lives of these children?"

Instantly Ruth angrily faced Marian. "What are you trying to do, torture her? Alva needs to put that place on the market. Everyone knows that! The property is nothing but a continual strain on her. Why shouldn't she be able to spend her last days in peace?"

Marian didn't have a chance to answer. Alva put her thin, veined hands over her face, and began to sob loudly.

The nurse who had kept on the fringes of the gathering hurried forward. "It's all right. It's all right. You're just overtired."

She gave Marian and Ruth a curt nod of dismissal. The tea party was over.

As they walked to the front door, the secretary made it clear that Marian was totally responsible for causing her employer's emotional breakdown. "I trust there'll be no further need for you to come here asking for more money. From now on, ask Mr. Kennedy to contact Mrs. Wentworth when necessary. If there is trouble of any kind at the estate, you can be sure we'll hold you responsible."

Any kind of trouble!

Marian left the cottage with the warning tolling in her ears. Walking back to the main building, she called Ryan's number at the station.

"Come and get me."

"Are you all right? Your voice sounds funny."

"Everything's fine," she answered quickly when, in truth, she felt like someone being carried full force into a whirlwind of disaster.

Chapter Eleven

Ryan left Scotty in good hands at the ranch.
His father beamed when he learned that the
boy was anxious to learn how to handle a
rope.

"I was a 4-H champion when I was your
age, Scotty," the older man bragged. "I could
rope a running calf quicker than you could
blink an eye. You've come to the right place,
buckaroo," he said as he patted Scotty on the
shoulder.

Ryan and his mother smiled as they
watched the two of them head out to the barn
with Laddie at their heels.

"You've made his day," Addie told her son,
smiling. "Your father gets a little restless now
that he can't handle the roundups the way he
used to. We miss having you around. I guess
police business keeps you busy? And other
things?" she asked as they walked to his car.

Ryan smiled. His mother was so obvious. She was wanting to know if there was anything personal going on between him and Marian. He'd never made a habit of bringing his dates around to the house. After he broke up with Joyce, he'd kept his romancing private. Bringing Marian home to meet the family might not have been such a good idea. He knew that his mother had expected that he and Joyce would be married by now and she'd happily have some more grand-babies to spoil.

The truth was, he didn't really have a clear-cut answer to give his mother. He just knew Joyce wasn't the woman he wanted as a lifetime mate. In contrast, the more time he spent with Marian, the more determined he became to pursue the deep attraction that aroused him every moment he was with her.

He ignored the question in his mother's eyes and thanked her for the hamper of food she always had ready for him when he dropped by. He didn't have the heart to tell her that the freezer compartment in his small refrigerator was chock-full.

"Will you give Scotty some lunch if it's past noon when we pick him up?" he asked as he got in the car.

"Sure. He seems like a really nice boy. It's good of you to take him under your wing."

Ryan just nodded. He wasn't about to share any information with his mother about the present situation. If Scotty got out of line, Ryan was confident his folks would handle it firmly and fairly. More importantly, he'd be safe in their care.

As Ryan drove back to town, he wondered what his police chief had thought about the skimpy report he'd hastily submitted the day before. Anyone else but the fifty-five-year-old Clyde Peterson would have pulled him in for a complete rundown on the situation requiring protective custody for an eleven-year-old boy. Luckily, Chief Peterson had confidence in his men or they didn't stay long on the force. He'd been the one to inspire Ryan to enlist in the Denver Police Academy in the first place, and then persuaded him to return to Rock Creek to serve the small community.

Ryan had never been sorry about the decision he'd made to stay close to his family roots. *What about Marian? Can you see a professional woman like her being happy living in a small cowpoke town?*

He pushed the unwelcome personal questions aside for the moment. Fortunately, he'd achieved this kind of mental discipline, and his ability to focus on the immediate had made him a good investigator.

As he hurried up the steps of the police station, he was mentally writing up his report. As soon as he had finished it, he'd take it to the chief himself.

He had just started to turn down the hall to his office, when he met Peterson's secretary, Alice Winters. She was a short, energetic woman who had been Peterson's right hand for nearly fifteen years. No one questioned her authority about anything.

"The chief wants to see you," she said in her usual brisk way.

"Thanks, Alice." He couldn't resist a slight grin in contrast to her solemn expression. "Am I in trouble?"

"Aren't you always?" she retorted. Any hint of affection she might feel for him softened her eyes for just a split second before she swung on the heels of her sensible oxfords and disappeared into the records room.

Ryan knocked politely on the slightly opened door of the private office.

"Come in!"

Ryan straightened his shoulders as he went in. Even though he wasn't wearing a uniform, he was expected to look like someone ready for inspection. "You wanted to see me, boss?"

Chief Peterson swung his chair around. He was a slender man with a mop of unruly graying hair. "I'd like to know whether we've got a crime to solve or just some kid's creative blarney."

"I haven't nailed anything down yet," Ryan admitted. "So far Forensics hasn't come up with much. We've got a fingerprint matching the caretaker's nephew, but he's a drifter and could have been at the cabin seeing what he could lift."

Peterson pursed his lips. "And that's all you've got?"

"There is one more thing that makes me want to stay on it a little longer. The cleaning ladies who routinely work at the Wentworth estate said that a Navajo rug is always placed in front of the fireplace. It was there when they cleaned the cabin before the summer education program began."

Peterson leaned forward in his chair. "And you're thinking…?"

"If there was a body there when Scotty broke into the cabin, it could have been on the rug. Then someone could have removed it with the body during the time that it took for Marian Richards, the director of the children's program, to find Scotty and call us."

"What does the boy say?"

"He doesn't remember the rug, but that's not surprising. Seeing a dead man would keep anyone from noticing, especially a kid."

"So where are we on this?"

"I want to continue the protective custody and investigation a little longer. If Scotty is in danger from a killer wanting to silence him before he does remember something incriminating, it's worth a few days of my time to prevent it."

Peterson rubbed his chin in a thoughtful manner as he leaned back in his chair.

Ryan remained quiet. He'd learned not to interrupt this thoughtful ritual no matter how long it took. Peterson would not be rushed into a decision, nor would he change his mind once it was made up.

When he finally looked up at Ryan, he nodded. "All right. Better safe than sorry on this. Wasting a few days of your time seems to be warranted if a boy's life may be at stake."

"Thanks, boss."

"Leave a written report about what we've just talked about. If I have anyone breathing down my neck about this, I want to have some official information on record."

Ryan nodded, headed for his office, and had just finished the report when the telephone rang.

It was Marian requesting he come and pick her up.

The tension in her voice made him think she hadn't gotten what she came after. "You bet. Give me ten minutes."

When he drove up and saw her waiting for him on a bench outside the front entrance of the building, a sudden spurt of masculine pleasure surged through him. He didn't understand why she totally attracted him on levels that had been missing in his relationship with Joyce and every other woman he'd met socially and professionally.

As she walked to the car and slipped into the front seat, he could tell that she was deeply disturbed. He resisted the temptation to pull her close and rest her head against his shoulder as he stroked the soft sun-tinted strands of her hair. Everything about her was beginning to touch him on a deeper level.

Even though the answer seemed obvious, he asked, "How did it go?"

She gave him a forced smile. Moistening

her lips and taking a deep breath, she replied, "Mrs. Wentworth authorized the hiring of the aide I wanted."

"And?"

"And what?"

"What went wrong?" he asked bluntly.

For a moment she looked as if she wasn't going to answer. Then she lifted her chin. "I made an enemy."

"An enemy? Who?"

"Her secretary, Ruth Tilman."

"Tell me what happened."

Marian drew in a deep breath. "We had a tea party. The conversation was pretty general at first, but that changed when Alva began talking about her grandson, Stanley. She became quite emotional about the fact that she'd disinherited him. When she started crying about her broken dreams of not seeing Stanley's children living on the estate, I felt sorry for her. Impulsively I invited her to come and see what a blessing it was the way her property was being used to change the lives of other children."

"And?" Ryan prodded when she fell silent.

"Her secretary went into a tirade!" Marian's jaw tightened. "She raved about how the property was a continual strain on

Mrs. Wentworth. She made it clear that she thought our program is a burden her employer shouldn't have to bear."

"She's just trying to throw her weight around," Ryan said, frowning. He didn't know the woman, but he'd bet Ruth Tilman was looking out for her own welfare.

"She warned me not to approach Mrs. Wentworth again. If she'd had the authority, I know she would have dismissed me right then and there. No doubt Mr. Kennedy is going to get an earful from her."

"He knows you've been doing a good job," he tried to reassure her.

"I'm not so sure he'd stand by me if he knew the police were investigating a possible homicide on the property involving one of the students." Marian drew in a shaky breath. "It's a good bet both he and Ruth Tilman would push to have me removed if there's the slightest notoriety connected with the estate."

Ryan swore under his breath. Keeping something like this completely under wraps for much longer was going to be difficult—especially if it turned into an official murder investigation. Even having put Scotty under protective custody wouldn't look good for the summer program, and parents might withdraw their children because of it.

He couldn't resist putting an arm around her shoulders and was surprised when she leaned into his embrace. "It's going to be okay. I'll do my best to see that you don't get hurt," he promised. "We've got Scotty pretty much under control now and no matter what happens in this investigation, I'm going to try to protect both of you."

He bent his head and let his lips lightly brush her cheek. He expected a stiffening, a quick intake of breath or some negative reaction, but when she turned her head to look up at him, he was almost convinced she wanted him to kiss her. Knowing that she was vulnerable at the moment, he was surprised at the protective feeling that suddenly swept through him. How could he start something that might end up only hurting her? Denying himself those half-parted, luscious, tempting lips, he placed a light kiss on her cheek.

If she was surprised or disappointed, she didn't show it as he drew away and put his hands on the steering wheel. "Let's get some lunch before we pick up Scotty. My mother said she'd feed him, and you deserve a little break."

"Oh, I don't know…" she said hesitantly, looking at her watch.

"My mother sent a hamper of food home with me. She seems to think I'd starve if she didn't keep my freezer and refrigerator full. We could have a quick lunch on my townhouse patio."

She hesitated and then agreed. "That might be faster. But I really need to be back at the mansion by the time the afternoon sessions begin."

BY THE TIME they reached his town house, one of several dotting a wooded hillside, Marian wondered if going to his place had been a good idea. Now that she had her emotions under control, she realized that she must have invited his tender overtures. In truth, she'd wanted him to hold her, even kiss her. But she was in control of herself now. She hoped she hadn't given him the wrong signals by agreeing to go to his place.

After parking beside his town house, he led the way into a small kitchen opening into a nice-size living room. French doors opened onto a small patio overlooking the town below.

"Nice," Marian said as she looked around the kitchen. "I like the red-checkered curtains."

"That's my sister's doing," he confessed. "In fact, Ellen is responsible for most of the decor. She has a similar town house in another unit."

"So she looks after you," Marian said with a smile.

"If you want to call it that," he replied without smiling back. As he began to unload the hamper, he said, "If you'd like to freshen up, the bathroom is just down the hall."

Nodding, she turned in that direction. As she passed the first small room off the hall, she peeked in and saw that he was using it as an office.

Placed under one window was a large, old-fashioned desk that might have been brought from the ranch. A couple of file cabinets stood against one wall. One rather faded easy chair and a footstool hinted that he might spend some time sitting there with his long legs stretched out and his head leaning back against the high cushion. Everything was unpretentious, exuding the same down-to-earth aura of his parents' ranch house.

Just a few steps farther down the hall was a small bathroom. Apparently his sister's decorating touch hadn't extended to the bathroom. No matching towels and washcloths. No fancy toothbrush holder and matching cup. A plain tan shower curtain and bath rug looked as if they might have been donations from the ranch.

One small shelf above the sink was crowded with masculine toiletries. Shaving cream, hair tonic and spicy lotion were there, teasing her with familiarity as she remembered faint whiffs of their scents as he had held her close. Her senses had been filled with the warmth of his nearness and for those brief moments, she had no longer been alone.

The feeling was a stranger to her. She had enjoyed masculine attention and companionship from time to time, but never had wanted to exchange them for her goal-oriented life.

Had that somehow changed? she wondered. Was she ready to bury her head against a protective shoulder like Ryan's and release some of her I-can-take-care-of-myself attitude?

As quickly as the thought crossed her mind, she rejected it. She certainly wasn't going to open herself up to any complicated emotions when her whole professional future was dangling by a thread.

As she quickly left the bathroom, she caught a glimpse of his bedroom at the end of the hall and decided it was as unpretentious as the other rooms. A bachelor pad, for sure.

When she returned to the kitchen, Ryan had a couple of trays ready to carry out to the patio. "Are you hungry?"

"Yes," she lied.

They seated themselves at a small oval table with wrought-iron chairs. When he poured her a small glass of white wine, she was surprised. It didn't seem like the kind of liquor a man would have around.

"Aren't you having any?"

He shook his head. "I just thought you might need something to whet your appetite a little. It's hard to eat when you're uptight."

She appreciated his sensitivity and after a few sips, the knots in her stomach eased enough for her to feel hungry.

"My mom's chicken is the best," he bragged. "And her green-bean mixed salad won an honorable mention at the county fair a couple of years ago," he added. "And for dessert, I hope you like macaroon cookies. Mom always packs enough to last me a month."

As they ate, she asked some questions about the history of the area and knew she'd touched a responsive chord when he eagerly responded with the spark of a history buff.

"Before the white man came along, Navajo Indians roamed this area. As kids, we used to hunt for arrowheads and I ended up with a nice collection. The town got its name from an early gold mine the prospectors called the Rock Creek Mine. A small settlement remained after the mine closed. Now it's mostly agriculture and ranching."

"It seems like a nice place," she replied rather too politely.

"I can't imagine that someone with your professional background would find much stimulation here," Ryan commented. "There's no college and only a very modest library. Those who want advanced degrees or higher training have to seek it elsewhere."

He paused, giving her the impression he was wanting some kind of personal commitment from her that these things didn't matter. But they did! She'd dry up and blow away without being able to use her education and experience.

Her silence seemed answer enough. As he rose to his feet, he said, "I guess it's time to pick up Scotty and get you back to the estate."

"Yes," she agreed. Picking up her tray, she followed him back to the kitchen. And then it happened! As she inadvertently bumped into the corner of the dishwasher, the jolt was enough to tip her tray and spill everything on the floor.

"Oh, I'm sorry!" she gasped.

Stooping down, she quickly began picking up the pieces of the broken wineglass. In her haste she nicked one finger and blood spurted from the cut.

"Let that go," Ryan ordered as he pulled her over to the sink and began running cool water over the cut. Then he reached into a cupboard and brought out a small first-aid kit with Band-Aids and a tube of disinfectant.

Embarrassed that she'd been so clumsy, she stammered, "I—I'm sorry. I've made a mess all over the floor."

"The first one ever in this kitchen, too," he replied with mock solemnity. "I guess I'd better do what my mother always did for me in a situation like this."

"What?"

He carefully lifted her hand and placed a kiss on the wounded finger. As he locked his deep blue eyes on hers, he asked softly, "Is one kiss enough?"

Her breath caught as he slowly put his arms around her waist and drew her to him. As she leaned into his inviting warmth, he bent his head and kissed her. Tenderly at first and then deeply, and possessively. His tongue caressed her lips as if he was drinking fully of the passion that was rising within her. She was lost to everything but the sensation of his kisses and the tender stroking of his hands. She wanted him to make love to her. She wanted—

She was startled when he suddenly stiffened and drew back. Then she heard the doorbell and the opening of the front door.

"Yoo-hoo, Ryan. I saw your car. Have you had lunch?"

As she walked into the living room and looked into the kitchen, Marian recognized her as the shapely blond woman who had kissed him that night at the mansion. Undoubtedly she was Joyce, the one Ryan's family wanted him to marry.

"Oh…oh," she stammered, her eyes widening. "Ryan, I didn't know you had company."

There was a hard set to his jaw as he walked into the living room. She couldn't hear what he said as he took Joyce's arm and walked her to the front door.

Coming back to the kitchen, there was a hard set to his jaw as he apologized to Marian. "I'm sorry about that."

She was surprised how steady her voice sounded as she replied, "Let's go pick up Scotty."

Chapter Twelve

Ryan's hands tightened on the steering wheel as he drove to the ranch. He was as angry with himself as he was with Joyce. None of this would have happened if he'd been more firm with her and with her constant attempts to be part of his life.

His high school romance with Joyce had been one for the books. They'd been the couple other students had envied. Elected king and queen for their graduating prom. Their families had smiled, whispered and openly encouraged the relationship. Even after Ryan had spent a couple of years away at police academy, and had dated other women, Joyce had been the "girl back home." She'd never left Rock Creek. Her feelings for him had stayed the same—but his had changed completely. She didn't understand or refused to accept that it was over.

He'd tried to remain friends with her but she was always pushing to recapture their romantic past.

As he shot a look at Marian's stiff profile, he silently swore. Her kisses had ignited deep longings he couldn't even define. He had wanted to carry her off to his bed, make love to her, and declare what was happening in his heart. Joyce had destroyed all that.

He reached over and took one of Marian's hands. "About Joyce, I want to explain."

"I understand," she replied evenly and she removed her hand from his.

"No, you don't."

"Please, let it go."

"No, I won't." He set his jaw. "Joyce and I have a history. A romance that ended long ago—only nobody will accept that. Not Joyce! Not our families! The town is so damn small that we're always included in the same activities. I'm guilty of just letting it slide."

"I'm sure you find her very attractive."

"Joyce is nice but too pushy. Like today." Then he added curtly, "And the evening you saw her kissing me good-night."

"Please, there's no need for any explanations. I'm not expecting a hot-and-heavy romance between us because of a few kisses. I'm not Joyce. I have a career that doesn't allow detours."

"Are you saying there's no place for a small-town detective in your life?"

"I guess that's what I'm saying."

"Well, I'm glad we got that straightened out."

"Better now than later, don't you think? I'll be going back to Denver at the end of the summer. I want to continue my work with educational programs for handicapped children." Her tone softened just slightly. "You've been very supportive and I don't know how I would have coped without you. But on a personal level—"

"Spare me the details. I get the message," he answered shortly.

THEY CONTINUED the rest of the drive to the ranch in silence. Marian didn't know how to recapture the easy relationship that had been between them before the kisses.

When they turned down the ranch driveway and the house came into view, she could see Ryan's mother and Scotty sitting on the porch swing.

When Ryan stopped the car in the front

driveway, Scotty jumped out of the swing. Ryan's mother handed him something and he came bounding down the front steps with a big smile on his face. Laddie leaped from where he was sleeping on the porch and dogged Scotty's footsteps to the car.

Marian couldn't see what the boy had in his hand until he came around to her side of the car. Scotty was clutching a small flower-pot planted with lavender violets.

She quickly opened her door, expecting him to thrust the flowers into her hands. Instead, he gave her a sheepish grin.

"See what I got for Mindy!"

"She'll love it," Marian readily responded. Joy shot through her as she looked at his beaming face. Was this grinning youngster the tough street urchin who didn't give a damn about anybody or anything?

"Way to go." Ryan nodded with approval. "Jump in the back with Laddie and we'll deliver it."

When his mother came over to the car, he rolled down his window. "Mom, I bet you've had Scotty out in your garden," he teased.

"That boy's got a green thumb for sure," she answered, making sure Scotty could see her lips. "Best helper I ever had."

"Did he wear Dad out?"

She nodded. "He said Scotty's almost ready to rope something that moves."

"Uh-oh. We better watch out for Laddie."

"You bring them back soon." As her gaze moved to Marian, she added, "Nice to see you again, Miss Richards."

"Thank you," Marian responded politely, and couldn't help wondering if his mother was regretting that it wasn't Joyce sitting in the front seat with her son.

On the way back to the estate, Scotty did most of the talking. Apparently the rope throwing with Ryan's dad had gone well. He bragged he could bag a fence post on the first try most of the time.

Ryan nodded and gave him a thumbs-up.

"I helped your ma plant some funny-looking stuff. She said I could shovel a hole in the garden faster than anybody."

As he chatted like a normal kid his age, Marian breathed a sigh of relief and prayed nothing would get in the way of the progress he was making.

LUNCH WAS JUST ENDING as they entered the house. The children were filing out of the dining room and heading upstairs for rest period. As soon as Scotty spied Mindy in the hall, he hurried to catch up with her.

He touched her shoulder and held out the pot of flowers. As she took them, he clumsily signed, "For you."

Her surprised look changed to a broad smile as she held out the flowers to show the other girls. They made the usual girlish giggles and, a little embarrassed, Scotty turned away.

At that moment, an older boy pointed at Scotty and then signed something that made his companions laugh.

Before either Marian or Ryan could react, Scotty lunged at him. He grabbed the mocking boy around the neck with one hand and pounded him with his fist with the other.

"Fight! Fight!" A chorus of excited cries rose to the vaulted ceiling.

Ryan shoved his way through the excited children, but before he could reach the two fighters, they bumped into a hall console table and sent a porcelain lamp crashing to the floor.

"Oh my God," Marian gasped.

"Break it up! Break it up!" Ryan yelled. They were unable to hear the order, but it was doubtful they would have stopped anyway.

Ryan had to physically separate the boys and put himself between them. "That's enough! Cool it!"

"He made a dirty sign," Scotty protested loudly, his hands still balled in a fist.

As if there wasn't enough confusion, Laddie began barking and dancing around Scotty as if he wanted to get in on the fun.

"Down, boy!" Ryan ordered.

At that moment, Nancy came out of the dining room and Rob came down the stairs at a run. Usually the movement after a meal from one location to another was an orderly one.

"What on earth happened?" Nancy gasped.

As succinctly as possible, Marian explained. She kept her voice even and under control, as though this wasn't the last straw in a perfectly horrible day.

Thankfully, the two teachers quickly took charge and herded the excited children up the stairs. Marian put her hand on the shoulder of the boy who'd caused Scotty's outburst, and motioned to Ryan to bring Scotty to her office.

Laddie trailed along, sniffing his way down the corridor as if a feast of smells was a dog's heaven.

After closing the door, she faced the two boys. The withdrawn scowl on Scotty's face made her heartsick. The progress they'd made in the last few days had visibly disappeared. The angry street kid was back.

She'd never had any trouble with Jeff before. He wasn't the smartest pupil they had and obviously he was just showing off by making fun of Scotty because of Mindy and the flowers.

Without putting the blame on either one, she signed as she spoke aloud. "This kind of behavior is not acceptable. Both of you need to show some self-discipline. You will spend time in the kitchen helping Elsie while you think about it. She'll set up a schedule for you."

Jeff's expression eased, but Scotty's cold stare told her he was hanging on to his anger.

"Would you like me to escort them to the kitchen to speak with her?" Ryan asked, giving her a smile of approval. "I'm going that way."

"Yes, please," she said gratefully, glancing at her blinking desk phone. "I probably have some calls to answer. And catch up on the morning's work."

"Sure thing." He motioned to the boys and waited until they were on either side of him before leaving.

THE DINING ROOM still needed cleaning up and Elsie was loading the dishwasher when Ryan brought the boys to her.

"I have a couple of boys who need to work off some misplaced energy," he told her.

"Yeah, I heard the hullabaloo." She rested her hands on her ample hips as she looked at each of the boys. "I reckon I have some pans that need scrubbing, a floor to mop and some corn to husk for dinner."

"That should do it." Ryan nodded in agreement. "Keep them here and busy."

The boys must have read Elsie's lips enough to know she planned on working them every minute. There was a hint of rebellion in Scotty's scowl, but Ryan was confident Elsie could keep him in line.

Ryan went out the back door and headed for the caretaker's apartment with the dog loping along at his heels. He quickly climbed the stairs and found the door of the apartment wide-open.

"Hello! Henry?" Ryan called, peering through the screen door. Some lunch dishes were sitting on the coffee table in front of the couch. A sandwich was only half-eaten and a beer bottle was almost full. An opened newspaper had fallen to the floor.

Everything about the scene spoke of hurried action. Had something or someone called Henry away while he was eating and reading the newspaper?

Ryan ordered the dog to stay outside and went inside.

"Henry?" He called the caretaker's name again.

Still no response.

Ryan quickly checked the bedroom and bathroom. Except for the usual clutter of a single man, nothing seemed out of place.

Ryan was puzzled. What could have happened to make Henry leave so abruptly?

Ryan left the apartment door the way he'd found it and went down the steps to have a quick look in the garage. Henry's pickup truck was parked in its usual place, so he must be on the premises somewhere.

With Laddie snooping his way past trees and bushes, Ryan circled the house. He couldn't see any sign that the caretaker had been working there. Had something unexpected taken him away from the house? To the cabin, perhaps?

Ryan was heading in that direction, when Laddie took off running toward the stable. The next minute he spied Henry moving around in the corral. There wasn't any livestock on the premises that Ryan knew of. He'd already made a quick check of the outbuildings when pretending to check out the security systems.

When Ryan reached the corral, he stepped up on one of the log railings so he could see over the fence. Henry had his back to him, piling some gunnysacks on top of what looked like a trash heap.

"Need some help?" Ryan called out.

Henry jerked around, his expression similar to a thunderstorm. He threw down the load in his arms and stomped over to the fence. "Oh, it's you!"

"You expecting someone else?" Ryan responded evenly.

"Hell, yes!" he swore. "I just got a call from Mrs. Wentworth's high-nosed secretary. In her holier-than-thou tone, Miss Tilman tells me that the old lady has decided the children ought to have some Shetland ponies to ride."

"Oh, oh," Ryan replied, instantly wondering what this might mean to his protective custody of Scotty. He wasn't about to let the boy go riding off by himself.

"The owner of the horses is coming out this afternoon to check on things. I'm to have the place ready for inspection. Just like that." He glared at Ryan. "You know what I think?"

"What, Henry?"

"I think the old lady is off her rocker and someone is trying to get ahold of this place."

"Really? What makes you think so?"

Henry's mouth curled up in an ugly smirk. "You stick around and you'll find out."

Ryan wanted to keep him talking, but Henry turned on his cowboy heels and stomped away, disappearing through the open door of the stable.

Thoughtfully, Ryan walked slowly back to the house. Glancing at his watch, he noted that it was almost time to relieve the boys of their duty. When he and Laddie went through the back door into the kitchen, he was surprised to see they were already gone.

"I worked their tails off," Elsie assured him. "Not a word of back talk from either of them. I let them leave ten minutes early as a reward for getting everything done. Jeff went upstairs with Rob, and I put Scotty in your room to wait for you. I told him if he moved one inch out of it, he'd have to help clean up in the kitchen for the next week."

She patted Laddie as she put down a plate of food for him. "Good dog." She'd made a pallet for the dog in the corner of the kitchen and Ryan was thankful she cared for him and didn't seem to mind at all when he got underfoot.

He left the kitchen and walked down the short hall of the servants' quarters. Ryan had made certain that the door at the end of the hall was locked and the key safely in his pocket.

The door to the room they had taken was shut. Ryan eased it open quietly. After the workout his dad had given the boy, Ryan wouldn't have been surprised if Scotty was ready to sleep the afternoon away.

Scotty's bed was empty. The pillow wasn't indented and the covers weren't ruffled as a sign he'd been napping. Everything seemed exactly the way they had left it that morning before going into town.

He strode across the floor and knocked firmly on the bathroom door. "Scotty! Are you in there?"

No response.

He quickly opened the unlocked door. Empty.

Dammit! Somehow Scotty had escaped without Elsie seeing him. He knew that Elsie had taken the first room closest to the kitchen. The rest of the servant rooms were vacant except the one he and Scotty were using.

Ryan walked down the hall and checked the outside door. Still locked. Now what? As he passed the closed doors of the remaining rooms, his nose caught a whiff of smoke.

Stopping abruptly, he began opening doors on one side of the corridor and then the other. The scent was suddenly stronger as he approached the room opposite Elsie's.

He swung the door open and there was Scotty sitting on the floor smoking a cigarette. For a split second, the scene didn't quite register, but as Scotty scrambled to his feet, Ryan reached out and grabbed his arm.

"Where'd you get the cigarettes?" His voice was as sharp as a cracked whip.

"I found them?"

"Where?"

"They're only butts," Scotty argued, trying to pull away.

Ryan leaned into his face. "Where did you get them?"

Scotty swallowed hard as he answered in a weak voice. "At the cabin."

"Where at the cabin?"

"They were in an ashtray. In the kitchen."

Ryan didn't know whether to shake him or kiss him as a neon light flashed in his head.

DNA. Cigarettes contained DNA.

Maybe they'd finally get some answers.

Chapter Thirteen

Marian was just hanging up the phone when Ryan and Scotty came into the office. She'd been talking to the local Teachers Placement Bureau, asking for the names of teacher's aides who might be interested in summer employment. She was pleasantly surprised when they gave her several referrals and was hopeful she'd find one who had an interest in her program.

Her smile faded when she looked up into the stormy faces of Scotty and Ryan. Both of them looked like thunderclouds about to break. What had gone wrong now?

"I've got to make a trip to the crime lab," Ryan told her shortly. "You'll have to keep an eye on Scotty while I run something to Toby at the lab."

His voice sounded tense. She waited for him to explain and when he didn't, she asked bluntly, "Has something happened that I need to know about?"

"I just found Scotty smoking some cigarette butts."

"What? I thought he was in the kitchen with Elsie? Where did he get them?"

"He says he found them at the cabin."

"And he didn't tell us?"

"I'm sure he doesn't have any idea how important they could be to prove who might have been in the cabin."

"Maybe he's lying. Maybe he got them some other place. I don't think Elsie or the teachers smoke, but they might. Scotty, come here!" She motioned the boy over to her desk. She looked him squarely in the eyes. "Tell me the truth. Where did you get the cigarettes?"

He scowled at her as he answered, "In the kitchen."

"Elsie's kitchen?"

"No." He looked at her as if she was being ridiculous asking such a question. "At the cabin."

"Where were they in the cabin?"

"I told him already," Scotty replied, glaring at Ryan. "In the ashtray."

"Why didn't you tell us before?"

He just stared at her without answering, but Marian knew the reason. Scotty didn't want to give them up. In his boyish mind he hid them from everyone because he knew they'd be taken away from him if anyone knew. He had no idea how vital the butts might be in making an identification of the person who left them in the cabin. When she looked at Ryan, he put into words what she was thinking.

"They might give us a DNA lead. Even better than fingerprints. I need to get them to Toby ASAP." Then he turned to Scotty and pointed to a nearby chair. "You sit there and don't move unless Marian says so. I mean it! Don't give her any trouble."

"He'll be fine," Marian quickly assured Ryan.

"I shouldn't be more than a couple of hours," he promised.

She was sure that she'd put their passionate lunchtime kisses behind her, but as she watched him walk away, a deep longing held a warning that she might be lying to herself.

Ryan took the steps into the police station two at a time. Then he quickly crossed the lobby and took an elevator to the second floor where Rock Creek's forensic laboratory was located. Even though it was modest in size compared to forensic laboratories like Denver's, it was fully equipped to follow similar procedures.

Ryan had found little need to go elsewhere when working a crime scene. Under Toby's direction, the lab offered an identification unit for revealing and enhancing fingerprints, a chemistry lab, a darkroom for developing film and an enclosed area for testing firearms and bullets.

Toby had only one assistant, Mattie, a rather unsociable, middle-aged woman who was standing at the lab counter when Ryan came in. She barely looked at him before resuming her work.

Ryan quickly walked to the far end of the laboratory and a sense of relief shot through him when he saw Toby sitting at a desk in a small glassed-in cubicle. This new development was too hot to keep to himself.

Ryan gave a light tap on the open door as he poked his head inside. "Are you open for business?"

"Depends on the business," Toby quipped, smiling. "You look like the proverbial cat that swallowed the canary."

"You better believe it."

"All right, give."

"I've got something for you."

"Okay."

Ryan reached into his pocket. "You're never going to believe it."

"Try me."

Ryan laid a plastic envelope on the desk.

"What is it?"

"Cigarette butts."

"Where'd they come from?"

"The cabin."

"The cabin?" Toby's eyes widened.

"From the kitchen."

"How'd we miss them?" Toby's expression was one of pure disbelief.

"We didn't. They weren't there," Ryan explained quickly. He knew how conscientious Toby was about his work. "Scotty lifted the butts from the ashtray and failed to tell us. I caught him smoking one of them."

"I'll be damned," Toby swore. He studied the cigarette butts in the envelope as if he were viewing pure gold. Then he grinned at Ryan. "Let's put these little babies to work."

Ryan followed him to the section of the lab where DNA testing was carried out. Like all other crime laboratories across the country, Toby used CODIS, a Federal Bureau of Investigation DNA database, to match samples with any DNA on record.

"We'll try the Colorado database first," Toby said as if reading Ryan's thoughts. "I'll try to send the pattern out as soon as possible." He gave Ryan his usual optimistic smile. "Who knows, we may hit a home run first thing!"

"I sure hope so. The chief is going to pull me off this if something doesn't surface."

"We're still running the fingerprints."

Ryan knew that fingerprints of all those in the military, as well as people in public service, like teachers, health-care workers, plus all those accused of any crime, created a current backlog of thousands of samples on record.

"I'm surprised you haven't found Henry Ziller's prints. I know they're on record. He was in the army as a young man when the Wentworths hired him to be caretaker."

"Nothing so far."

"Well, work your magic."

"Will do. How is everything going with the director?" Toby asked as he walked out into the hall with Ryan.

"Not as well as I'd like."

Toby chuckled. "Until I saw her in the hall

with you, I didn't know she was so young and good-looking."

"She is that."

"And?"

If it had been anybody but Toby, Ryan would have ignored the invitation to share his feelings. The two of them had been on a lot of demanding cases together and their relationship was deeper than just a business one. Ryan took a deep breath. "Marian is the most sensitive, caring and purposeful woman I've ever met. At the same time she's utterly feminine and totally sexy without even trying."

"Uh-oh," Toby said, shaking his head. "I think I get the idea. You've fallen for her."

"In a big way, I'm afraid."

"So what's the problem? Don't tell me she's indifferent? Not to a tall, dark and handsome male like yourself."

Ryan remembered the way her hungry mouth had accepted his kisses and the tantalizing way her body had leaned into his. She had responded with every ounce of her being. His voice was a little husky from remembering as he assured Toby, "She's not indifferent."

"Then what's the problem? What's holding you back? You're overdue for a hot-and-heavy affair."

"It's not an affair I want," he answered shortly. "I think this could be the real thing. She's everything a man could ask for in a mate. She's great with children. Affectionate, loving. Any man would be proud to have her as a wife."

"Okay, you've got me convinced. What's holding you back?"

Ryan shook his head. "Marian's ambition and goals don't fit a hick town like Rock Creek. She'd be miserable, I know."

"No, you don't know anything of the kind. Never make the mistake of trying to predict what a woman's thinking or feeling. Maybe she's so focused on her career because the right man hasn't come along. Your best bet is to let her know how you feel." He gave Ryan a slap on the shoulder. "Go for it."

With a wink and a grin, Toby turned away and walked back into the lab.

MARIAN'S AFTERNOON had been filled with preparations for the Mesa Verde field trip. So far, so good. Enough groceries had been ordered for Elsie to make up the necessary sack lunches. Marian had scheduled interviews in the morning for the new aide who would be able to help chaperone.

There was one big blessing in all of this and she clung to it. The bus would be filled to capacity with students, teachers, the nurse and the new aide. More than enough adult supervision without her.

Ziller had come bursting into the office earlier, ready to explode.

"I suppose this is some of your doing," he lashed out. "It isn't enough that the place is being overrun by kids. Now I've got to take care of a half-dozen horses. Do you know how much work—"

"What in the world are you talking about?" She quickly interrupted his tirade. "Horses?"

"Shetland ponies. Don't tell me you didn't know."

"Know what?"

"The old lady's secretary called me. I've been ordered to get the stables ready for a half-dozen ponies for the kids to ride."

"Oh, no." Marian sighed as she leaned back in her chair. She remembered the conversation with Alva about her grandson, Stanley, and his love of riding, but nothing was said about buying any horses for her summer program. "Honestly, Henry, I'm as surprised as you are. Really, I am."

He just snorted as if he knew a lie when he heard one. Turning on his heel, he stomped out.

Marian stared unseeingly at the papers on her desk. Oh, no! She could just imagine Kennedy's reaction when he heard about a stable of Shetland ponies being added to the current expenses. She made up her mind right then and there that he was the one who would have to confront Alva.

Before she changed her mind, she called his office in Denver. When his secretary answered, she recognized Marian's name.

"Oh, yes, Miss Richards. I'm sorry, he's not in today but I'll put you on his call-back list. Or would you like to leave a message?"

"No, thank you. I'd rather speak with him directly."

A few minutes later, when Marian heard footsteps coming down the hall, she quickly brushed her hair back from her face and straightened up in her chair. What else could happen today?

Ryan politely rapped on the open door as he peered in.

"Still at it, huh?"

She nodded. "Just about ready to wrap up."

"Where's Scotty?"

"He's with the nurse. Bertha took one look at him and decided it might be a good idea to check him over. She's been after him to clean his plate at meals and so far hasn't had much luck. Apparently, he's quite a few pounds under the recommended weight." Marian paused. "I didn't tell her about the cigarettes or anything."

"Good. I guess I was a little hard on him."

"I can understand why you were, but I don't think it does any good to put him on the defensive. No telling what else he might be able to tell us if he doesn't feel threatened." She added, "I doubt that any kid would voluntarily admit he had some cigarette butts stashed away."

"I guess I'm a little too impatient sometimes," he admitted as he eased down on the corner of her desk beside her chair. "About other things, too."

As his deep blue eyes searched her face, she knew she wasn't ready for this conversation. She could feel her heart suddenly pulsating, the palms of her hands suddenly moist. It was too soon to bury the heated passion of his kisses, to forget the caressing hands that had stroked her. She forced herself to pretend she didn't know what he was talking about.

"What things?" she asked, hoping he'd bring up some mundane subject that would allow her to hold on to her composure.

"You and me."

"What about you and me?" she countered, as if offense was the best defense.

"You're not going to deny what happened between us today, are you?"

"Oh, I know what happened." She gave him a false smile. "I'm afraid I had too much wine. You know, dropping my tray like that. Cutting my finger. I'm afraid things got a little out of hand, that's all."

"Do you always lie to yourself like that?"

"I'm not lying."

"I dare you to let me kiss you right now."

She pushed her chair back and stood up. "Sorry, I've got some things to do."

"Are you running away from me? Please, Marian. Let's talk."

"This isn't a good time. You'd better check on Scotty and I'll see you at dinner."

"How about after dinner? Maybe we could find a few minutes to ourselves."

"Maybe," she replied as she headed out of

the office. Instead of going to the kitchen as she had intended, she headed for her apartment.

After closing the door quickly behind her, she leaned up against it and took a couple of deep breaths. It wasn't like her to run away from a problem, but she'd never dealt with one like Ryan Darnell. Her usual clear thinking turned fuzzy when he was around. She didn't know what to do with a rising conflict that just being around him created. Heaven knows, this was one time in her life when she needed to keep a clear head.

Slowly walking over to one of the deep cushion chairs, she dropped down into it, leaned back and closed her eyes. Surely she knew better than to let her emotions run rampant. Common sense told her she had to get a handle on this bewildering situation right now. Falling in love was not an option.

Falling in love?

She immediately rejected the idea. She had just met Detective Darnell. Their life patterns were about as far apart as any two people's could be. It must be the demanding circumstances that made her vulnerable to his kisses and caresses. No way was she going to lose her head and commit herself to a dead-end relationship. She had given him the wrong message. She was only going to be at the mansion for a few weeks. Once the program ended, she'd be moving back to Denver. She'd be miserable trying to fill her life in a small town like Rock Creek.

As she rose to her feet, she decided to take the coward's way out and not have dinner with the others. Several times when she'd had some demanding work to finish, she'd eaten a light snack in her room. Tomorrow would be soon enough to level with Ryan and make sure that what happened in his apartment was not repeated.

She heard the children going into the dining room as she kicked off her shoes and settled on the couch. She'd just bitten into an apple, when there was a knock at the door. She stiffened as she called out, "Who is it?"

No answer.

On occasion, a staff member would send a message to her with one of the older kids if she was needed for some reason. As the knock came a second time, she got to her bare feet and opened the door.

Ryan stood there. He was holding a tray of food and had a napkin folded over his arm like a waiter. With a slight bow, he said, "Your dinner, mademoiselle."

Before she could say anything, he walked past her and with a flourish set the tray down on the coffee table beside her half-eaten apple and cheese crackers.

She didn't know whether to laugh, get mad or go along with the charade. Even though she struggled to deny it, he made her forget all the reasons she wanted to keep some distance between them.

"You really shouldn't have—" she started to protest.

"When you didn't show for dinner, Elsie told me that you sometimes eat a little something in your room. She suggested I bring a tray and join you."

"What about Scotty?" she asked as they eased down on the couch.

"Oh, he's at the dining room table with the nurse. Bertha was determined to see that he eats every bit. When I told her you and I needed a couple of hours to consider possible changes in the security system, she offered to make sure he doesn't take off again."

"Do I detect a conspiracy?" she asked.

"Whatever do you mean?" he asked, feigning innocence.

"Elsie suggests you bring me a tray. Bertha volunteers to babysit Scotty. And you are completely innocent of orchestrating the whole thing."

"Well, maybe a little guilty," he admitted. "Let's eat and then we can talk about it."

"All right," she agreed, unable to resist his persuasive charm. "I didn't ask you what happened at the crime lab."

"Toby was excited about the find. If we get a DNA match, we may have the answer to a lot of things." He shared some experiences he'd had on cases that had been solved because of forensic investigations. "But let's not think about that now."

She was surprised when he picked up their empty plates and took them over to the sink. When he sat down again beside her, he took her hand. "We have to talk."

As the warmth from his touch tingled on her skin, as evenly as she could, she asked, "About what?"

"Us."

"If it's about what happened, I told you it was the wine."

"Really?"

Before she could protest, he had drawn her close and kissed her. Not a demanding kiss.

Just a soft tugging at her lips as his mouth captured hers. Unexpectedly a deep yearning seeped through her. She knew that she should pull away before it mounted into an uncontrollable need. As his kisses deepened so did her desire.

When he slowly lifted his head, and lightly traced her face with his fingertips, he said, "I don't think it was the wine. Do you?"

She managed a weak smile. When he pulled her close against him, she curled up in his arms as if she'd been waiting her whole life for this moment. He kissed her again and again and until their passion grew and she would have willingly lain beside him in Alva's fancy canopy bed.

She couldn't believe it when he slowly removed her arms from his neck and moved out of her embrace. No concealing the fact that he was as aroused and ready and willing as she was.

"What's…what's the matter?" she stammered.

"This is not what I want."

She moistened her suddenly dry lips. "And just what is it that you want?"

He searched her face. "I want more. I'm

ready for a commitment—a lifetime commitment. I want a home with someone who loves me and children who bear my name. And I want a wife who is beautiful, intelligent, sensitive and so sexy I can't live without her. Now that I've found her, I don't want to let her go." His deep eyes bore into hers. "Do you know what I'm asking you, Marian?"

She felt as if the floor had dropped out from under her. "This is way too sudden!"

"I know and I don't want an answer now. We have the whole summer to develop a lasting relationship. I just wanted you to know from the start that I'm totally serious about having you in my life."

Marian wasn't used to making any kind of decision without careful consideration. They'd only known each other for a few days and under the most trying and emotional circumstances. They had already talked about how limited the area was in the things that mattered to her. Even as she searched for words to explain, he nodded and drew away from her. "It's all right. I understand."

"I just need some time—"

"I moved too fast." He stood up and gave

her a weak smile. "Well, you can't blame a country boy for trying."

Then he walked out the door and closed it firmly behind him.

Chapter Fourteen

The next morning right after breakfast, Ryan left the house with Scotty and the dog.

He'd spent most of the night turning over in his mind everything about the present situation that didn't make sense. Putting aside his personal quandary over Marian's rejection, he concentrated on finding ways to move ahead with the investigation while waiting for Toby's report on the DNA.

Scotty's possession of the cigarette butts indicated that the boy might have more information lodging in his head that he wasn't even aware of.

"We're going to take a hike, Scotty. I want you to show me how you went to the cabin."

"Okay," he replied with his hands, and smiled at Ryan's obvious surprise.

As Scotty pointed toward the stream, Ryan knew that the boy had followed it through the trees until the cabin came into view on a slight knoll above the water. Finding the cabin must have been a surprise. There wasn't any way Scotty could have known it was there because it was hidden from all directions.

As they approached it, Ryan stopped and made Scotty face him. "Tell me everything you did that day."

Scotty pointed to a cluster of trees and bushes. "I hid there."

"Why?"

"I didn't want anyone to see me." His tone told Ryan that he thought it was a stupid question.

"Did you think someone was there?" Ryan prodded.

"Maybe."

"Did you see any movement around the cabin?"

He shook his head. "It looked empty."

"Did you see any sign of a car or truck anywhere?"

He shook his head again.

"Then what?"

"I walked to the front door and knocked."

Step by step, bit by bit, Ryan's questions took Scotty through every tiny remembrance of that day without revealing anything significant that they didn't already know.

The only positive revelation came when Ryan pretended to be the one who Scotty might have heard walking around the deck as the boy was leaving the cabin. He had instructed the boy to run the way he had before when he heard any vibration of footsteps.

Ryan had not quite reached the back corner of the deck when he glimpsed the back of Scotty fleeing through the nearby trees. What made his heart leap was the instant realization that Scotty's blond hair and slight build was easily identifiable by anyone standing there.

If Ryan had doubted the wisdom of his protective custody of the boy, all doubts were washed away at that moment.

They had just returned to the mansion, when Ryan received a call from the crime lab. It was Toby's assistant on the line.

"Toby wants you to come in this afternoon," Mattie said.

Ryan's heart jumped a beat. If CODIS had run all night maybe they'd gotten a hit already. "What's happening?"

"He'll be back about one o'clock."

Ryan knew he wasn't going to get a crumb

of information from her. "All right, Mattie. I'll be there."

Marian wasn't in her office when he stopped in to tell her what was happening. Their conversation this morning had been very reserved and neither of them had crossed the barrier that had risen between them. It was as if they were strangers instead of two people who had lost themselves in each other's arms.

Frankly, he didn't know how to recover the relationship that had been there before he completely overwhelmed her. He had really dropped the ball with his proposal that they spend their lives together. He realized he'd let his feelings get way ahead of his common sense. She wasn't at the same place in her life as he was. Now he would have to backtrack and restore a friendship—if she'd let him.

He left a note on her desk that he and Scotty would be gone for most of the day. He threw caution to the wind and added, "Can we talk when I get back?"

MARIAN HAD BEEN showing the newly hired teacher's aide, Mrs. Downing, around most of the morning. The woman had been a secretary before marriage and Marian was confident she could handle the time-consuming preparation of materials that would ease the teaching load for Nancy and Rob.

When Marian returned to the office and found Ryan's note, she realized that the emotional confusion his proposal had created had not subsided one bit. The truth was, she was being pulled in so many directions that her usual rational, unemotional approach to a problem wasn't working at all.

When the phone rang and pulled her out of her reverie, she took a deep breath as she answered, "Marian Richards."

"You called me?"

Her mind went blank for a moment when she heard Kennedy's voice. Then she remembered. The horses.

"Maybe you know all about this, but I wanted to check," she began.

When she told him about the caretaker's telephone call and Mrs. Wentworth's decision to buy a half-dozen Shetland ponies for the stable, a momentary dead silence answered her question. He didn't know.

"Where'd she get a fool idea like that?"

Marian certainly wasn't going to bring up Alva's comment about her grandson and his pony. "It was a shock to me, too. Perhaps you can change her mind, Mr. Kennedy, before it's too late."

"Not likely," he replied shortly and hung up with a crisp goodbye.

Her phone rang again and she kept busy the rest of the morning making final preparations for the Mesa Verde field trip.

RYAN AND SCOTTY had lunch with his mother—which turned out not to be a good idea. She was too damn perceptive. Always had been.

"Marian couldn't come with you today?" she asked as they had lunch on the patio with Scotty and Laddie.

"No, she's busy."

"She must have her hands full."

"Marian is the most capable woman I've ever met. No pretense about her at all. I imagine people misjudge her because she looks as good as any beauty queen—and doesn't even try." He started to say more, but the way his mother was looking at him stopped him.

"You really like her." She said it like a statement, not a question.

"Yes, I do."

"And?"

Ryan shrugged.

"Does she know how you feel?"

Giving his mom a wry smile, he replied, "I think that's the trouble. I came on a little too strong."

He quickly changed the subject and asked about the rest of the family.

"Gotta go," he said a short time later as he looked at his watch. "I have an appointment at one o'clock."

He had been uneasy about leaving Scotty when Marian was so busy. He didn't trust anyone else to keep a close eye on him. "You'll keep close tabs on Scotty until I get back? I didn't want to leave him when he begged to come."

"Sure. Don't worry about him. Your dad will be back from town any minute. The two of them make quite a pair."

"Thanks, Mom." He gave her a quick kiss and left.

When he drove into the parking lot at the police station, he saw that Toby's van was parked in its reserved space. A hopeful expectation made his steps long and quick as he made his way inside the building.

The habitually slow elevator increased his impatience. When he finally reached the crime lab, he forced himself to take a couple of deep breaths.

Toby saw him coming and turned away from the monitor he'd been viewing. He motioned for Ryan to follow him into his office. Then he closed the door.

"Maybe you'd better sit down for this one."

"Give," Ryan ordered and remained standing.

"We got a match on the DNA. Stanley Wentworth."

"Alva's grandson?" Ryan sat down then and mentally came at the information in a dozen ways, but none of it made sense. "There's no question?"

"None. His DNA is on file because of a high school scandal."

Ryan nodded. "I remember it. Just before his grandmother disinherited him a few years back, Stanley was falsely accused of fathering a teenage girl's baby. Turned out that the girl was guilty of trying to take him for a bundle."

"Apparently he's back in town."

"Without anyone knowing it?"

"So it seems," Toby replied. "The cigarettes were fresh."

Ryan's deductive mind wrestled with

myriad unanswered questions. Why would Stanley Wentworth be at the cabin? Was he meeting someone there? Someone he ended up killing? Or was Stanley the dead person Scotty found lying on the rug?

Chapter Fifteen

Ryan had decided that if anyone knew Stanley was in Rock Creek, it would likely be his grandmother. Stanley's DNA turning up at the cabin presented a hundred and one puzzles and not one of them made sense.

As he headed for the nursing home, his mind began shifting some of the possibilities this new evidence presented. Unfortunately, the more he analyzed the situation, the more convinced he was that he wasn't on the right track regarding any of them.

At the Sunny Acres Complex he showed his badge to the receptionist and was given Alva Wentworth's cottage number without any delay.

As he walked across the grounds, he tried to empty his mind of any preconceived notions. He knew it was never a good idea to go into an interview expecting to reinforce his own ideas or conclusions. He needed to be open and listen to whatever was said and later put it all in some kind of frame that would make sense.

He knocked briskly and the door was opened by a young nurse. Frowning, she said, "Yes?"

Giving her his best people-management smile, Ryan replied, "I would like to speak with Mrs. Wentworth."

"I'm sorry, she only has visitors by appointment."

Ryan could tell she was used to giving this automatic response. He drew out his badge once again. "This is official business."

The young woman's eyes widened as her gaze went from the badge to his face. "Maybe you'd better wait until Miss Tilman gets here."

"I don't think that's a good idea. In fact, I think it would be easier on Mrs. Wentworth if I talked with her alone, without her secretary."

She nodded as if agreeing that things were always easier without the secretary around. She motioned for him to come in. "Mrs. Wentworth is in the sitting room."

"Will you inform her that an old friend of her grandson, Stanley, is here to see her?"

Ryan followed the nurse to the door of the room and then waited until she had bent over the elderly lady and repeated what Ryan had asked her to say.

An expression of delight instantly showed in her wrinkled face. As she looked toward the door, her eyes sparkled with eagerness. Ryan experienced a stab of guilt, knowing that her joy was totally misplaced.

Walking over to her chair, he smiled and said, "I knew your grandson when we were in school together. My name is Ryan Darnell. What good times we used to have spending overnights at the cabin."

"You like my Stanley?"

"Yes, but I haven't seen him for a long time."

"He's been away, but he's coming back to stay." She leaned forward and whispered in her shaky voice, "Nobody knows. Only me."

"You've heard from him?"

"Not yet, but he's coming, and—" She stopped suddenly as her secretary entered the room.

"I didn't know any visitors were scheduled for today," she said briskly, glaring at Ryan. "I'm Ruth Tilman, and you are…?"

"Ryan Darnell. An old friend of Mrs. Wentworth's grandson."

"Really?" she replied with obvious skepticism.

Alva spoke up rather timidly. "Ruth, I told him I've forgiven Stanley and he's coming back."

"Is that what this is about? Have you been in touch with Stanley?" The woman's gray eyes narrowed as she glared at Ryan. "The nurse said you showed her a badge. Is Stanley in trouble again?"

Ryan gave the kind of noncommittal look that she could take either way.

"Hasn't he caused his grandmother enough heartache? We don't need to have her upset because he's gotten crosswise of the law again. What's he done now?"

Ryan deliberately sidestepped her question with one of his own. "How long has Stanley been back in Rock Creek?"

She drew herself up and gave him an icy look. "I'm not comfortable discussing private family business."

"It's my business," Alva unexpectedly protested. "The estate belongs to me. I can do with it what I like." Alva added with childish eagerness, "I've made up my mind to forgive him."

"Why? You haven't seen your grandson in years," Miss Tilman replied.

"You don't know everything," Alva retorted. "I don't care if he does want to sell the place."

"Is that what Stanley plans to do?" Ryan asked with an innocent smile.

She gave him a childish, cat-that-ate-the-canary look. "Maybe. Maybe not."

Ryan mentally groaned. It wasn't going to be easy to figure out how much was fact and how much was wishful thinking on her part. Had she seen Stanley or was all of this just senile wandering?

"It's time for your medicine and nap," Miss Tilman declared, cutting short anything more that Alva might say. "I'll ring for the nurse. I think you've had enough visiting for now."

Ryan knew it wouldn't do any good to try to prolong the interview. "It's been nice to see you, Mrs. Wentworth. I admire your courage," he told her.

He left the room and passed the nurse in the hall as she headed for the sitting room. Instead of letting himself out the front door, he eased down into a hall chair. He was rewarded by the secretary's shocked and irritated expression when she came out of the sitting room and saw him there.

"I thought you'd gone."

"I know," he replied smoothly. "I thought maybe you and I could have a private chat."

"What about?"

"Stanley Wentworth."

"I don't have any idea what I could say about him that would be of interest."

"Really? You've never met him?"

Her eyes narrowed as if she was deciding whether or not to agree with or deny the statement. "Of course I've met him. I came to town on another job while he was still living with his grandmother. In fact, he was the one who introduced us."

"So you were pretty close friends?"

She evaded a direct answer. "I only knew him a short time before things blew up with his grandmother and he left town."

"Alva seems to think he's either back or coming back."

"She's delusional. Most of the time she can't distinguish between her daydreams and reality."

"I see. So he doesn't know his grandmother has forgiven him and is ready to change her will?" Ryan could tell he'd hit a live button when he saw her stiffen.

"As I told you before, I don't discuss

personal family business. Unless you tell me exactly why you're here, this conversation is over."

Ryan nodded. "Yes, well, thank you for your time." He needed to have a little more to go on before pushing her any harder.

ONCE BACK at the office, he reported the new developments to Chief Peterson.

"All we know for certain is that cigarettes with Stanley Wentworth's DNA were left in the cabin. We can assume he was there. The next question is, why? Was he alone? Was he meeting someone? If so, who and why?"

Peterson nodded. "Judging from the guy's past actions, he can't be up to any good. Maybe we can do a little sniffing around town and see if he's contacted anybody lately. I'll put some cops on it."

Ryan nodded. "I'll contact some of the state agencies for any information on Stanley's whereabouts these last few years."

"Well, stay on it." He eyed Ryan thoughtfully. "You still think the kid is in danger?"

"I took Scotty to the cabin and checked out his story. Someone standing outside on the deck could have identified him as he ran away."

When Ryan returned to his office, he

began making calls to state agencies. He kept remembering that Alva had said Stanley was coming. He wondered if she'd hired someone to look for him.

MARIAN WAS SITTING on the back steps watching Rob put the children through some simple calisthenics when Ryan came back with Scotty and the dog.

"Can we take a walk?" he asked. "I need to talk to you."

"Sure." From his businesslike tone she knew he wasn't intending to pass the time with light conversation. Her heart tightened. What now?

After telling Scotty to get in the line with the others, she asked him, "Where do you want to go?"

"How about down by the stream?"

She nodded.

As they walked across the open area toward the water, she searched his face. They hadn't spoken about anything personal since those passionate embraces that had ended so abruptly. Over and over she'd replayed in her mind what had happened and wished she'd handled things differently. Common sense told her it was better to be honest now than later, but a mocking voice kept taunting her.

Do you really know what you're giving up?

When they reached the water, he motioned to some nearby boulders. "Have a seat."

The sound of the flowing water was soothing to Marian as they sat down. Neither of them spoke for a couple of minutes and she could tell from the set of his jaw that something was worrying him.

"What is it?"

"You're not going to believe it."

"At this point, I'll believe anything."

"Would you believe that Stanley Wentworth smoked those cigarettes?"

"Alva Wentworth's grandson?" Her mind refused to grasp the significance at first. "You mean, he was the one who scared Scotty and—"

"Killed somebody?" Ryan finished for her. "Until we have more answers we won't know if he's the murderer or the victim."

"What do you do now?"

"Try to find Stanley. Verify that he's still alive. I have the feeling that Ruth Tilman knows a hell of a lot more than she's saying."

"None of it makes sense."

"Most puzzles don't when there's a piece missing." He reached out and touched her shoulder. "Don't look so worried. Hang in there. How are preparations going for the field trip? That's tomorrow, isn't it?" Ryan frowned. "You're the one who has to tell Scotty he isn't going. I suppose it will be one more disappointment in his young life, but it can't be helped. In fact, I think we need to be even more diligent than ever keeping him close until I get more info about Stanley's whereabouts."

"Everyone will be gone tomorrow until late afternoon. I guess I'll have to keep him amused." Marian sighed.

"If you'll let me borrow your office, I can make some calls in the morning and then we could have our own outing." He snapped his fingers. "We'll make the day up to Scotty. There's an old Indian hunting ground not far from here. I'll drop a few arrowheads around and let him find them. He'll have something to show the rest of the kids when they get back."

"That would be wonderful." Impulsively, she leaned up and gave him a quick kiss on the cheek.

"Careful now," he warned as he put an arm around her. "You ought to know by now what one kiss can lead to."

"Is that a threat?" she asked him recklessly.

"No, that's a promise."

She could tell from the way his gaze caressed her face that he meant it.

Chapter Sixteen

Ryan made a quick trip to his town house the next morning while everyone was at breakfast. Quickly, he packed some fresh clothes in his carryall and changed into jeans and a favorite western shirt, and put on his cowboy boots. As he looked through a small box holding his collection of arrowheads, he could just imagine the delight on Scotty's face when he found the ones Ryan was going to drop around the old Indian hunting grounds. He was sure that collecting them was going to be a bigger thrill for the boy than the field trip would have been.

By the time Ryan got back to the estate, the children were being loaded onto the bus. Elsie was making sure the hampers of food were carefully stored, and Rob, Nancy, Bertha and the new aide were seeing that the children were safely buckled in. Henry was already in the driver's seat, waiting impatiently.

When Ryan saw Marian and Scotty standing on the porch watching the departure, he quickly joined them. Scotty's angry expression showed how he felt about not getting to go with the others. He glared at Ryan as if he knew it was him and not Marian who was responsible for making him stay behind.

Marian looked frazzled, as if she'd been anxious that everything was in order for the trip. "What's the old saying, if anything can go wrong, it will?" She sighed audibly as the bus drove away.

"I prefer the one that says, every cloud has a silver lining." He turned to Scotty and, reaching into his pocket, took out a key chain that had an Indian arrowhead dangling from it. Showing it to the boy, he said, "I found this arrowhead where Indians used to go hunting. Not far from here. Would you like to go there and hunt for some real Indian arrowheads?"

Scotty's expression changed like magic. His eyes widened as he quickly glanced at Marian.

Smiling, she nodded. "We'll take the lunches Elsie fixed for us and have a picnic."

Scotty's mouth spread in a boyish grin and Ryan could almost read his thoughts. *Wait till I show those guys some real Indian stuff.*

"I have a couple of hours' work and then we'll go," Ryan said.

"How far is it?" Marian asked. "Will there be much hiking?"

"No, we can take the car. There's a lumber trail off Canyon Road only three or four miles north of here. It's kind of rough but passable and drops down into a flat area cupped by nearby foothills. There's also a small lake. The Indians used to hunt there because deer and elk came down from the rugged mountainside to drink."

Marian's expression eased as she put her hands on the boy's shoulders. "Let's go get ready."

Ryan headed for Marian's office and used her phone and computer to put out a network of inquiries about Stanley Wentworth. Some of the data he got back was too dated to be significant and it might take days or even weeks to get new information. When he'd exhausted his resources, he glanced at his watch and decided he'd let it go until later in the day. He hoped Peterson would have better luck on the local scene. Stanley couldn't have materialized out of nowhere. He had to leave tracks somewhere.

As he left Marian's office, he was ready to

clear his head with some fresh air and exercise. He was pleased to find Marian, Scotty and the dog in the kitchen, ready to go.

Marian had changed into hip-hugging jeans, a snug red-and-white striped pullover, and she was wearing some sturdy hiking boots. With her hair tied back with a scarf, she looked almost as excited as Scotty. Good, he thought. The outing would relieve some of the stress she'd been under. Nothing like spending time in the outdoors, breathing in clean mountain air.

"Okay, let's do it. What can I carry?" He pretended to be shocked when Marian motioned to a pile of food containers, bottled drinks and a blanket. "All this stuff?"

"Don't worry, I bet we'll need every bit of it."

Laughing, he said, "Okay, let's go."

When they turned off the paved road a few miles north of the mansion, a forestry road began to climb a rugged hillside dotted with huge boulders and thick drifts of aspen and pine trees. When they reached the crest of the hill, they could look below and see a small lake in the center of a lush meadow.

They parked near the water for their

picnic. As Marian began to spread out their lunch, Ryan talked about the wild animals that used to graze there.

"Even bobcats?" Scotty asked eagerly, as if he'd seen one in a magazine or mounted in a museum.

Ryan smiled and nodded. "And mountain lions, too."

"That'll be enough," Marian chided. "I want to sleep tonight. It's lovely," she added, leaning back on her arms and looking around. "I'm surprised there aren't a lot of people here."

"About the only ones that find this place are hikers."

"I like to hike. You probably won't believe it, but when I was a teenager, I was a member of a Colorado hiking club. Not that I've climbed any of the really high peaks. Then my studies at the university and my career put an end to it."

Glimpsing this side of her suddenly renewed Ryan's hope that maybe they had at least one thing in common. "The La Plata Mountains are close by. Maybe we could do a little climbing before the summer's over?"

Before she had a chance to respond, Scotty declared pugnaciously, "Time to go hunting."

"Yes, it is," Ryan agreed as he stood up and

pointed. "I think the best bet is along the edge of those trees."

Scotty started out in that direction with Laddie at his heels.

"Good hunting," Marian said. "I think I'll take a hike around the lake."

"Good idea. That's just about the right distance to get your hiking legs back under you." He gave her an encouraging grin. "If you can't make it back, just give me a wave and I'll come carry you piggyback."

"Don't tempt me," she teased.

She watched as he and Scotty walked away together, the dog bounding along ahead of them. She was pleased with the companionship that was developing between Ryan and Scotty. Even when they were some distance away, she could see Scotty's jubilant response when he found one of the arrowheads Ryan had secretly tossed ahead when the boy was looking in a different direction.

As Marian made her way around the lake, she momentarily felt free of the heavy responsibilities of her position. She loved working with children like those in the program who needed so much help surviving in a fast-paced modern society. She knew her dedication was a deep part of her and she'd never willingly give it up. Still, it was a welcome tonic to hike along the edges of a deep blue mountain lake and lift her eyes toward the snowcapped peaks along the horizon.

She returned to their picnic spot just after Ryan and Scotty got there. As the two of them stood there, waiting for her to reach them, her sense of happiness startled her. Spending time with someone like Ryan touched her in ways that were both comforting and disturbing. She remembered how reassuring his solid body had been when he'd held her close and how the warmth of his full mouth on hers had made her forget everything else. Even now, as she watched him walk toward her, she stilled a foolish impulse to run into his arms and say, "Hold me!"

Fortunately the spell was broken when Scotty ran to her. Showing her the flint arrowheads he held in his hand, he said excitedly, "See, see what I found?"

"Terrific. Good job," she praised him as she gently cupped his head between her hands and spoke slowly.

"Now Scotty can start his own collection," Ryan said in the same deliberate way, facing Scotty so he could read his lips.

"I'm thirsty," Scotty declared, plopping down on the blanket.

"I told you we wouldn't have much to take back," Marian teased as they finished up the food and drink.

They had relaxed for about ten minutes when Scotty said suddenly, "Where's Laddie?"

Ryan and Marian looked around. Usually he plopped down somewhere close by. There was no sign of him.

"Laddie! Laddie, come here, boy!" Ryan called.

Marian expected to see a brown dog running toward them at full speed with his tail wagging. They stood up and searched the area around the lake and along the rocky line of trees.

Oh, no, she thought. Surely nothing could have happened to him. He wasn't very big. Suddenly she felt sick to her stomach.

"Maybe he went back to the car," Ryan said, turning in that direction and covering the ground in his wide stride. They had parked just off the rutted road in an open space that might have been made by forestry equipment at some time.

When he reached the car with Scotty close behind, he quickly saw that the dog was nowhere in sight. Dammit, Ryan silently swore. It wasn't like Laddie to take off on his own.

"Laddie! Laddie!" he shouted again. This time there was an answering bark from somewhere in the nearby cluster of trees. "Come here, boy!"

He waited a moment, called again. Still no dog.

"Stay by the car," he said to Scotty.

Silently muttering, Ryan pushed through a thicket of wild bushes and a stand of white-trunk aspen. When he saw a flicker of Laddie's tail and the sound of digging, he swore. "What in the hell?"

His nose told him what it was even before he saw the arm and hand that Laddie had uncovered. For a long moment Ryan just stared at the shallow grave. Half covering a body was part of a woven Indian rug.

Kneeling down, Ryan carefully lifted an edge of the rug. A stab of recognition was instant.

He'd found Stanley Wentworth.

Chapter Seventeen

As Ryan stood up, his thoughts whirled like a helicopter blade. Was this the body Scotty had seen on the rug? All the inquiries he'd put out to find Stanley Wentworth's whereabouts had now been answered. He was the victim. Someone had dumped his body here the day Scotty had been at the cabin.

He pulled Laddie back and ordered him to sit. Then, as carefully as he could, Ryan walked around the perimeter of the grave. One area of the rug was already exposed by Laddie and his digging.

He was just about to turn away and go back to the car when he saw something shiny caught in a fold of the rug. He knelt down and stared at it.

They were the fancy cuff links that Arthur Kennedy always wore!

Even though Ryan had been stunned

before at the unbelievable outcome of some of his cases, he'd never had such a climactic jolt as this one. He didn't know what motive the Denver lawyer had for committing the murder, but there wasn't any doubt in Ryan's mind that he would find one to prove his guilt. Seemed the lawyer was a very smart killer.

Very carefully he removed a cuff link with a tissue, staring at it for a long moment in the palm of his hand before turning away and making his way back to the car. His mind raced. First he had to call Toby, get the forensic investigation on the scene before any evidence could be destroyed.

Marian was waiting at the car with Scotty when he returned with Laddie.

"Oh, you found him," she said, smiling as Scotty rushed forward with a welcome hug for the dog.

"And something else, too," he said as he held out the tissue and showed her the cuff link.

She stared at it for a long moment. "It looks like—"

"Yes," he said before she could finish. "Let's go. I'll tell you more in the car."

As Ryan turned the car around and headed back to the mansion, he knew there was no easy way to tell her about the ugly discovery. He was glad Scotty couldn't hear their conversation. He decided short and quick was the best way to handle the matter.

"Laddie found a grave. The body was wrapped in an Indian rug."

Her whole body went stiff and she stared at him with an expression of total disbelief. He knew her well-ordered life had not prepared her for this kind of emotional upheaval. "There's something else," he added quickly. "I'm sure it's Stanley Wentworth buried there."

"How can you be sure?"

"I recognized him."

"You're saying that…that…"

"Arthur Kennedy unwittingly left his calling card," he finished for her. "The cuff link must have caught on the rug when he moved the body. He probably didn't miss it soon enough to know where he lost it."

As color faded from her face, he wished he'd waited to tell her when he could have taken her in his arms, but there wasn't time. He had to notify Chief Peterson immediately and have him call the Denver authorities to hold the lawyer for questioning. Getting Toby on the scene as quickly as possible was vital. He didn't want any scavengers to spoil the open grave.

As soon as they reached the mansion, they all piled out of the car and Ryan lightly put his arm around her as they entered through the kitchen's back door.

"I'll make the calls from your office."

"We'll be in my apartment," she replied in a ragged voice.

"Yes, rest if you can." He held her close for a long minute and brushed a kiss to her forehead. "It's going to be all right. Trust me."

With Scotty and Laddie trailing her, she disappeared down the hall.

The empty mansion echoed with his footsteps as he hurried to Marian's office. The place was like an eerie tomb without the noise and bustle of the children.

Ryan quickly made his two calls and was fortunate to reach both men immediately. He reported his findings to Chief Peterson, who agreed that the Denver authorities should be notified to pick up Kennedy and hold him for questioning.

"Yes, I know where the old Indian grounds are," Toby assured Ryan when he heard about the grave. "I'll leave now with Mattie and we'll meet you there. After I see what the situation is, we'll notify the coroner."

Ryan hung up and glanced at his watch. Almost two o'clock. He knew he should get back to the grave site as soon as possible, but he couldn't leave without making sure Marian was going to be able to handle the total shock of realizing her immediate boss was a murderer.

She was sitting motionless on the couch when he came into the room. Scotty was sitting on the floor, arranging his arrowheads, and Laddie greeted Ryan with his wagging tail. He quickly sat down beside her and put his arm around her shoulders. "I know this is mind shattering for you, but you can handle it. Believe me, the shock will soon wear off. What time is the bus due back from the field trip?"

She moistened her lips. "About five o'clock."

"Good. You stay here and rest until then. I'll be back as soon as I can." He tipped her head so he could look into her eyes. "I love you."

She moistened her lips. "I love you, too."

The kiss he gave her was a promise. "Hold that thought until I get back."

She nodded and gave him a weak smile as he left the room.

"Where's he going?" Scotty asked.

"To work," Marian replied.

"Can we go arrowhead hunting again? I bet I could find lots more."

Marian knew that she never wanted to go near those hunting grounds again. She'd never thought of herself as a coward, but all she wanted to do was run away and not be a part of the horror that had suddenly engulfed her. Her mind refused to accept any of the statements that Ryan had voiced so calmly. How could Arthur Kennedy, the lawyer who had worked with her to create the summer program, be a murderer? It couldn't be true. Nothing about him revealed that kind of vicious nature. He was too civilized. If the dead man was Stanley Wentworth, why would Alva Wentworth's lawyer want to kill him?

"I'm thirsty," Scotty complained, breaking into her tormented reverie. "You got something to drink?"

"How about milk?"

She ignored his frown and walked over to the small refrigerator. Glad to have something to do, she poured a glass of milk and was taking a couple of cookies out of a bag when she heard footsteps coming down the hall.

Was Ryan back already?

She swung around and nearly dropped the glass of milk. Standing in the doorway was Arthur Kennedy. She didn't know what to do. There was no place to run. No one to call.

She just stood there as Laddie bounded over to him, giving a few barks that sounded like a welcoming committee. His tail wagged as he sniffed the expensive, polished shoes and danced around the pressed trousers.

Kennedy gave the dog only a glance as his eyes settled on Scotty sitting cross-legged on the floor. "I thought he'd be on the field trip with the others."

Marian couldn't think of any kind of reply. Her mind was too filled with recent happenings to offer any kind of explanation. She started to say something about the boy not feeling well as Kennedy walked over to where she was standing.

"I expected you to be in your office, catching up on some work while you had a little peace and quiet. I knew you didn't go with the others. I met the bus when it arrived at Mesa Verde."

"Why?" she asked.

He glanced over at Scotty but didn't reply to her question. As Marian followed his gaze, her stomach took a sickening plunge. Had he been planning on using the field trip as a way to rid himself of a possible witness to his being at the cabin when he murdered Stanley? When the boy hadn't been with the others, had he driven back to the mansion to find him?

Surely Scotty's lack of any reaction to him must have reassured Kennedy that the boy he'd seen fleeing the cabin had not seen him. Marian began to breathe a little easier. She didn't think the lawyer would invite any more violence if he could avoid it.

"We were just going to have some milk and cookies. Will you join us?"

"Don't you have anything else?" He glanced over at the bar. "Alva used to keep that pretty well stocked."

Marian knew there were two unopened bottles of scotch left in the cupboard. Surely he wasn't going to stay! If he would just leave and go on believing that his crime had not been discovered, the police could catch up with him.

When Kennedy walked over to the bar and took out one of the bottles, she knew he wasn't going to leave without having a drink or two. She had to keep up the pretense that nothing had changed in their relationship, even though every minute in his presence was going to be pure hell.

"It's perfectly all right to have a social drink now and again," he assured her in that authoritative tone of his as he poured her a drink, too.

She prayed he didn't notice her sweaty palm as she took the glass. She was glad when he didn't sit on the couch beside her but took a nearby chair. All she had to do was keep her head and he'd have his drink and leave.

There was no warning when Scotty finished his milk and cookies and got to his feet. He came over to Kennedy's chair and showed his arrowhead collection to the lawyer.

"See what I found?"

Kennedy's eyes narrowed slightly as he mouthed, "Where?"

Marian tried to deflect Scotty's answer, but she failed.

"Where the Indians used to hunt. They were all over the ground."

"When?"

"This morning. Ryan found something, too." Scotty pointed to one of Kennedy's cuff links. "One of those. Didn't he, Marian?"

Kennedy was on his feet in an instant. His drink fell to the floor as he jerked Marian to her feet. "You lying bitch!" His hands bit into her shoulders as he shook her. "Play me for a fool, will you?"

He hit her hard enough across the jaw so that her knees crumbled and she fell like a rag doll. He pulled her up and was about to hit her again when Scotty started pounding Kennedy on the back with his small fists.

As he loosened his grip on Marian and turned to make a grab at Scotty, she cried, "Don't hurt him! Don't hurt him!"

"Somebody help!" Scotty cried as he ducked a blow aimed at his head.

There was such a ringing in Marian's ears, she thought she was imagining Ryan's voice. Then she saw him coming through the doorway, gun in hand.

"You bastard!" he yelled. "One move, Kennedy, and you're dead!"

As the room began to whirl, Marian gave in to the weakness she felt. As she lay there fighting not to lose consciousness, she felt Laddie licking her face.

Chapter Eighteen

When Marian woke up the next morning, she stared at the unfamiliar ceiling of Ryan's town house and then sat up quickly as yesterday's climactic scenes came rushing back.

Her chest tightened when she remembered how Ryan had handcuffed Kennedy and immediately called for backup. He'd made Scotty and her stay in her apartment until two officers took the lawyer away in a patrol car just before the bus returned with the children and staff.

After Ryan had quickly explained the situation to Bertha and the teachers, the nurse immediately checked Marian to make sure she was all right.

"I'm fine," Marian had lied in a shaky voice.

Ignoring her, Bertha had made her swallow a couple of tranquilizers. The nurse agreed with Ryan that Marian needed to get away from the mansion until the shock had worn off.

Scotty would be fine, Ryan had assured her, happily showing off his prize arrow-heads to everyone. Bertha had promised to keep him in tow. The danger that had hung over his head was gone.

By the time they'd driven to Ryan's town house, the pills Bertha had given her had begun to do their job. Her muscles had relaxed, her thinking had slowed and she hadn't protested when Ryan tucked her in his bed for a nap.

Now the room was dark, with only a small glow from a night-light, and she had no idea how long she'd slept. As she put her bare feet on the carpet, she remembered Bertha had packed her an overnight bag and she'd changed to her shortie pajamas before getting into Ryan's bed.

As she went across the hall barefoot to the bathroom and turned on the light, she glanced at her watch. It was almost two o'clock in the morning. She wondered where Ryan was sleeping.

Leaving the bathroom, she went into the hall and glanced in the room that was his office. It was dark. The living room was softly lighted and the television was on low. When she saw him stretched out on the couch, she thought he was asleep. As she came closer, she was surprised when he instantly sat up.

Smiling, he held out a hand and eased her down on the couch. "Hello, sleepyhead."

"I can't believe I slept all afternoon and evening."

"How do you feel now?"

"Back to normal."

"That's what I want to hear."

When she turned her head and looked into his eyes, she saw such tenderness and concern there, she knew that whatever she had to give up, she wouldn't and couldn't let him go.

He'd already made it plain that he wanted her in his life, but she'd let her pride and ambition overshadow the miraculous gift he offered. Since it was not in her nature to delay acting on any decision she made, she said evenly, "I love you, Detective Ryan Darnell."

His eyebrows lifted. "Does this mean…?"

"I'm saying yes, if it's not too late?"

"No, it's not too late, Miss Richards."

He gently put his arms around her and drew her close. As he kissed and caressed her, her whole body yearned with an unbelievable hunger. She didn't know what the future held, but for the moment she only wanted to give herself to this man in a way she'd never experienced before.

Then he carried her back to the bedroom and as they lay naked together, they made love as if coming together was a miracle that had almost escaped them both.

A WEEK LATER, Marian received a call in her office from Ruth Tilman, advising her that Alva Wentworth wanted to see her.

"Two o'clock this afternoon," the secretary informed her in her usual crisp tone.

"I'll be there."

Marian had heard the wealthy widow was taking her grandson's murder very hard and using her wealth and prestige to express her rage in all kinds of ways. No doubt, heads would roll, and Marian suspected that hers might very well be one of them. Undoubtedly, Alva would be critical of the way she had kept back the truth about Scotty being under protective custody, without informing her of Ryan's investigation into Scotty's story. Looking back, she was grateful that Ryan's presence had probably kept Kennedy from approaching the boy directly. No telling what Scotty's innocent reaction would have been, but it could have easily gotten him killed.

The foundation board for hearing-impaired children had met in Denver to debate what should be done about the summer program in light of the murder charges against Arthur Kennedy and the death of Alva Wentworth's grandson.

When Ryan showed up at noon to have lunch with her and Scotty, she told him about her appointment with Alva.

"I'll go with you. No need for you to put up with any chastising from her."

Ryan had been successful in establishing the lawyer's motive. Arthur Kennedy had almost persuaded Alva Wentworth to sell the property at the end of the summer. Because the Denver lawyer was on the inside of a land scheme that would make the Wentworth estate a prime location for a new ski-area development, Kennedy was in the position to know there was a fortune to be made in a southern Colorado resort.

When Alva changed her mind about forgiving Stanley, and making him her heir again, she told Kennedy. The lawyer located Stanley and arranged for a private talk with him at the cabin. He offered to help Stanley put all the legalities of his inheritance in place before his grandmother and anyone else knew he was back in Rock Creek. Then Kennedy carried out his plan to kill him and dispose of the body, but he hadn't realized his lost expensive cuff link had tied him to the murder.

Marian knew that Ryan had been right all along to make sure Scotty was protected. Whatever happened at her meeting with Alva, she had no apology for having believed in Ryan. Everyone on her staff knew she had fallen in love, but she didn't mind their knowing smiles when they saw her and Ryan together. She was confident she could weather any criticism and blot on her professional career because she'd found something much more important—the love of her life.

When they reached the nursing home, Ryan walked with her to Alva's cottage and he gave her a reassuring smile as they waited for someone to answer their knock.

When the door was opened, Ruth Tilman gave them a curt nod and stepped back to let them in.

"Nice day," Ryan said in a cheery tone that only increased her frown.

Marian's tension instantly eased. She didn't have to worry. Whatever happened, Ryan would be there to help her handle the situation. This reliance on someone else was completely new to her. All her life she'd fought her own battles and had the scars to prove it. Now she was able to smile and nod at the unfriendly woman without even a quiver of apprehension.

Alva Wentworth was sitting in her usual chair, wearing another expensive robe with elaborate lace trimmings. Marian thought her posture seemed straighter and her gaze more direct than before. She acknowledged their greeting and motioned toward the nearby sofa.

Marian expressed her sympathy immediately. "We're sorry for your loss, Mrs. Wentworth." She couldn't even imagine the heartache the woman must be feeling.

Alva nodded her gray head in acknowledgment as she waved her secretary from the room. "And tell the nurse not to bother us." Then she reached over and picked up some papers on the table beside her chair.

Ryan squeezed Marian's hand and she squeezed it back.

They both knew that if Alva had decided

to end the summer program and close up the mansion, Marian's reputation as director would suffer. It wasn't fair, but that's the way the academic world sometimes worked.

Her voice was a little raspy as she handed Marian the papers. "I've made the proper legal arrangements and have advised your official board that I'm deeding my property over to the Colorado Foundation for Disadvantaged Children, complete with an endowment for a year-round program."

Marian stared at the papers, and the fine print blurred as tears edged into the corners of her eyes.

Alva's mouth curved in a satisfied smile. "I hope this will meet with your professional plans, Miss Richards, and you will remain as director."

Marian nodded, so moved she was unable to say more than "Thank you."

"You're a very smart and generous woman, Mrs. Wentworth," Ryan said. "This will be a legacy that all of Colorado will truly value and your name will be honored because of it."

They left shortly after that. Marian felt like laughing and crying at the same time.

Ryan was obviously jubilant. "I've got something to show you to add to the celebration."

Marian didn't know where they were going and didn't care. Her mind was already leaping ahead to what the challenge of a year-round curriculum and staff would entail. It wasn't until Ryan had stopped the car that she realized they were parked in a lovely mountain area close to town.

Ryan pulled her gently from the car. "I've been wanting to buy this property for a long time. And I finally did it."

He took her hand as he began describing his dream. "The house would go over there, against the backdrop of those tall pine trees. And there's a meadow for a barn and plenty of room for Scotty and Laddie to run. The stream isn't far away for good fishing. Over here, on an evening, there's a colorful view of a sunset behind those snow-covered peaks."

A soft breeze ruffled her hair as he swung her around to face him. "A boy like Scotty could grow up here and you'd be close enough to get to the mansion easily." He searched her face. "What do you think?"

As she slipped her arms around his neck and drew him close, she whispered, "I think it's home."

* * * * *

Look for
LAST WOLF WATCHING
By Rhyannon Byrd
The exciting conclusion
in the **BLOODRUNNERS** *miniseries*
From Silhouette Nocturne

Follow Michaela and Brody on their fierce
journey to find the truth and face the
demons from the past, as they reach
the heart of the battle between
the Runners and the rogues.

Here is a sneak preview of book three,
LAST WOLF WATCHING

Michaela squinted, struggling to see through the impenetrable darkness. Everyone looked toward the Elders, but she knew Brody Carter still watched her. Michaela could feel the power of his gaze. Its heat. Its strength. And something that felt strangely like anger, though he had no reason to have any emotion toward her. Strangers from different worlds, brought together beneath the heavy silver moon on a night made for hell itself. That was their only connection.

The second she finished that thought, she knew it was a lie. But she couldn't deal with it now. Not tonight. Not when her whole world balanced on the edge of destruction.

Willing her backbone to keep her upright, Michaela Doucet focused on the towering blaze of a roaring bonfire that rose from the far side of the clearing, its orange flames burning with maniacal zeal against the inky black curtain of the night. Many of the Lycans had already shifted into their preternatural shapes, their fur-covered bodies standing like monstrous shadows at the edges of the forest as they waited with restless expectancy for her brother.

Her nineteen-year-old brother, Max, had been attacked by a rogue werewolf—a Lycan who preyed upon humans for food. Max had been bitten in the attack, which meant he was no longer human, but a breed of creature that existed between the two worlds of man and beast, much like the Bloodrunners themselves.

The Elders parted, and two hulking shapes emerged from the trees. In their wolf forms, the Lycans stood over seven feet tall, their legs bent at an odd angle as they stalked forward. They each held a thick chain that had been wound around their inside wrists, the twin lengths leading back into the shadows. The Lycans had taken no more than a few steps when they jerked on the chains, and her brother appeared.

Bound like an animal.

Biting at her trembling lower lip, she glanced left, then right, surprised to see that others had joined her. Now the Bloodrunners and their family and friends stood as a united force against the Silvercrest pack, which had yet to accept the fact that something sinister was eating away at its foundation—something that would rip down the protective walls that separated their world from the humans'. It occurred to Michaela that loyalties were being announced tonight—a separation made between those who would stand with the Runners in their fight against the rogues and those who blindly supported the pack's refusal to face reality. But all she could focus on was her brother. Max looked so hurt…so terrified.

"Leave him alone," she screamed, her soft-soled, black satin slip-ons struggling for purchase in the damp earth as she rushed toward Max, only to find herself lifted off the ground when a hard, heavily muscled arm clamped around her waist from behind, pulling her clear off her feet. "Damn it, let me down!" she snarled, unable to take her eyes off her brother as the golden-eyed Lycan kicked him.

Mindless with heartache and rage, Michaela clawed at the arm holding her, kicking her heels against whatever part of her captor's legs she could reach. "Stop it," a deep, husky voice grunted in her ear. "You're not helping him by losing it. I give you my word he'll survive the ceremony, but you have to keep it together."

"Nooooo!" she screamed, too hysterical to listen to reason. "You're monsters! All of you! Look what you've done to him! How dare you! *How dare you!*"

The arm tightened with a powerful flex of muscle, cinching her waist. Her breath sucked in on a sharp, wailing gasp.

"Shut up before you get both yourself and your brother killed. I will *not* let that happen. Do you understand me?" her captor growled, shaking her so hard that her teeth clicked together. "Do you understand me, Doucet?"

"Damn it," she cried, stricken as she watched one of the guards grab Max by his hair. Around them Lycans huffed and growled as they watched the spectacle, while others outright howled for the show to begin.

"That's enough!" the voice seethed in her ear. "They'll tear you apart before you even reach him, and I'll be damned if I'm going to stand here and watch you die."

Suddenly, through the haze of fear and

agony and outrage in her mind, she finally recognized who'd caught her. *Brody*.

He held her in his arms, her body locked against his powerful form, her back to the burning heat of his chest. A low, keening sound of anguish tore through her, and her head dropped forward as hoarse sobs of pain ripped from her throat. "Let me go. I have to help him. *Please*," she begged brokenly, knowing only that she needed to get to Max. "Let me go, Brody."

He muttered something against her hair, his breath warm against her scalp, and Michaela could have sworn it was a single word.... But she must have heard wrong. She was too upset. Too furious. Too terrified. She must be out of her mind.

Because it sounded as if he'd quietly snarled the word *never*.

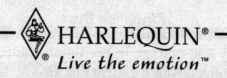

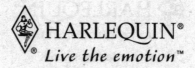

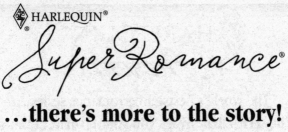

HARLEQUIN®
Super Romance®

...there's more to the story!

Superromance.
A *big* satisfying read about unforgettable
characters. Each month we offer *six* very different
stories that range from family drama to adventure
and mystery, from highly emotional stories to
romantic comedies—and much more! Stories
about people you'll believe in and care about.
Stories too compelling to put down....

Our authors are among today's *best* romance
writers. You'll find familiar names and talented
newcomers. Many of them are award winners—
and you'll see why!

If you want the biggest and best
in romance fiction, you'll get it
from Superromance!

Exciting, Emotional, Unexpected...

HARLEQUIN®
Live the emotion™

HARLEQUIN® Presents®

**The world's bestselling romance series...
The series that brings you your favorite authors,
month after month:**

Helen Bianchin...Emma Darcy
Lynne Graham...Penny Jordan
Miranda Lee...Sandra Marton
Anne Mather...Carole Mortimer
Susan Napier...Michelle Reid

and many more uniquely talented authors!

Wealthy, powerful, gorgeous men...
Women who have feelings just like your own...
The stories you love, set in exotic, glamorous locations...

HARLEQUIN® Presents®

Seduction and Passion Guaranteed!

HPDIR104